my parents are sex maniacs...

by
Robyn Harding

annick press
toronto + new york + vancouver

Annick Press Ltd.

Edited by Pam Robertson
Copyedited by Heather Sangster
Proofread by Helen Godolphin
Cover and interior design by Black Eye Design / Grace Cheong
Cover illustration by Monika Melnychuk

We acknowledge the support of the Canada Council for the Arts, the Ontario Arts Council, and the Government of Canada through the Book Publishing Industry Development Program (BPIDP) for our publishing activities.

ONTARIO ARTS COUNCIL
CONSEIL DES ARTS DE L'ONTARIO

Cataloging in Publication

Harding, Robyn

My parents are sex maniacs : a high school horror story / Robyn Harding.

ISBN 978-1-55451-179-2 (bound).—ISBN 978-1-55451-178-5 (pbk.)

I. Title.

PS8615.A715M9 2009   jC813'.6   C2008-906369-4

Printed and bound in Canada

Published in the U.S.A. by	**Distributed in Canada by**	**Distributed in the U.S.A. by**
Annick Press (U.S.) Ltd.	Firefly Books Ltd.	Firefly Books (U.S.) Inc.
	66 Leek Crescent	P.O. Box 1338
	Richmond Hill, ON	Ellicott Station
	L4B 1H1	Buffalo, NY 14205

Visit our website at www.annickpress.com

Sienna and I are sitting cross-legged on my lavender bed-spread while our parents are downstairs having after-dinner drinks. My mom cooked a special meal to celebrate Sienna's mom, Sunny, winning Sifton Realty's salesperson of the year award. As soon as we'd finished our beef bourgui-gnon and roasted potatoes, we absconded to the privacy of my bedroom. I'd wanted to hang around for the raspberry cheesecake, but Sienna doesn't really do dessert.

"So," I say to my best friend, who is staring at the tips of her French manicure, "do you want to work on our designs?"

Sienna and I are going to become fashion designers when we finish high school. We're going to move to New York, where she'll attend Parsons School of Design (she has a flair for fashion) and I'll go to the School of Visual Arts (I have natural artistic ability). We'll share a small apartment until we get our degrees, then we'll move into some enormous loft space in Nolita and launch our empire.

Sienna shrugs. "I'm not really in a very fashion design-y mood."

"... Okay. Do you want to look at some of the designs I did for our label instead?" We'd spent many hours trying to find the right name for our business. Since we are about to become the next Dolce & Gabbana (except, obviously, we're not gay Italian ex-lovers), I'd suggested Harrison & Marshall. But we'd both agreed it didn't have much cachet. My next idea was a combination of our first names: Louise and Sienna—LouSi. I still think this is kind of clever, but Sienna prefers Sienna Lou. She thinks it has a sort of Daisy Duke appeal.

I kneel on my off-white carpet and extract the large sketch pad I keep hidden under my bed. It's not that I'm ashamed of my drawings; I'm actually quite proud of the work Sienna and I have done. It's just that we've decided to keep our fashion empire plans from our parents and class-mates so it will have more impact when we make it big in New York. I also don't want my younger brother, Troy, to find them. He'll totally make fun of our designs, and I don't need him messing with my fragile artist's ego.

Flipping through the sketch pad, I stop at a brightly col-ored page. "These are the Sienna Lou designs," I explain, handing the pad over. "And I threw in a few LouSi's...just for fun, I guess."

Sienna glances briefly at the curlicues of the first logos, her eyes flitting over the more angular, modern versions. There is an unmistakable expression of indifference on her lightly tanned, flawless face. She pulls her blue eyes away and looks at me.

"What do you think of Dean Campbell?"

The question is somewhat jarring. I mean, we're talking about our *label* here—our life's passion, our calling, our *future*! With some effort, I mentally conjure the swarthy, weather-beaten face of Dean Campbell. What do I think of him? The short answer is: I don't. Dean Campbell is *old*. I'm not sure how old, but his dark stubble gives the impression he could grow a full Santa Claus–style beard if he wanted to. I also have a feeling that the Von Dutch trucker hat he always wears is hiding a receding hairline.

"Why?" I ask, troubled by Sienna's interest in him.

She shrugs. "I don't know. I saw him at McDonald's last night and we kind of had a . . . thing."

"A *thing*?"

"Like a look. You know . . . a *moment*."

Ewww! I don't say this out loud, however. Instead, I say, "Isn't he going out with Tracey Morreau?"

Sienna shrugs again. "I hear they're having problems."

"How old is he?" I ask as nonchalantly as possible. I don't want to sound childish. Despite the fact that Sienna and I are both sixteen, she seems at least a couple of years older. This is probably because she's had a body like Pamela Anderson's since she was about twelve. I've recently developed smallish breasts, but let's face it: no one is going to be hiring me to jog in slow motion in a bathing suit any time soon.

Sienna says, "I think he's, like, twenty-four or something."

"God! That's practically thirty!" Oops. My cool facade has slipped. I try to cover. "That's like . . . just a *little* bit old for you, don't you think?"

My best friend rolls her eyes. "Tracey Morreau's only seventeen and she's going out with him."

"Yeah, and Tracey Morreau is a total skank!"

Sienna laughs. "True. But there's something kind of *exciting* about an older guy, don'tcha think?"

"I guess," I say, completely unconvinced. Though Sienna and I have both spent our entire lives in the suburban community of Langley, she seems to have a maturity and sophistication I lack. This could be because of her enormous boobs—or maybe it's my mother's dictatorial supervision of my television and movie viewing? Whatever the reason, I guess I'm still too juvenile to see the appeal of a guy who is already going bald.

Suddenly, my bedroom door bursts open and I quickly flip my sketch pad over to conceal our logo designs. Troy is standing in the doorway with Sienna's kid brother, Brody, slightly behind his stick-thin form. Troy addresses Sienna. "Your parents are leaving."

"'Kay," she says, staring at her manicure.

"Okay!" I yell as my fourteen-year-old brother lingers in the entryway. "We heard you. Good-bye!" It's revolting how Troy takes any opportunity he can get to ogle Sienna.

Troy's eyes narrow as he glares at me. "Fat bitch," he says venomously.

"Get lost!" I shriek, hurling a tissue box at him. Troy closes the door in the nick of time. "God," I say to Sienna, "brothers are so annoying."

"Yeah." She gets off my bed. "At least my brother's practically mute."

Slowly, Sienna and I make our way downstairs to where our parents are gathered near the front door. My mom is handing plastic containers of food to Sienna's father, Keith. My dad is helping Sunny into her white rabbit-fur coat. "Just heat the meat up right in the wine sauce," my mom is instructing. "You can microwave it, but I find it tastes better if you put it on the stove and let it simmer for a while."

"Are you getting all this, Keith?" Sunny says to her husband. I can hear the gin and tonics in her voice. "You know my talents don't lie in the kitchen."

"Oh, really?" my dad asks suggestively, hands on her rabbit-covered shoulders.

"Why, Len Harrison," Sunny says, slapping at him playfully. "I had no idea you had such a dirty mind. I meant my talents lie in the *office*, of course. Get your mind out of the gutter!"

Sienna shoots me a look and rolls her eyes. We hate when our parents get tipsy and make these sorts of pervy comments.

"Of course... the office..." My dad plays along.

"That's a good idea." Sienna's dad gives his wife a randy wink. "We should try out some of your *talents* in the office."

"Well," my mom says a little awkwardly (thankfully, she is not as depraved as the rest of them), "you don't get to be the number-one salesperson for Sifton Realty without talent."

"Why, Denise Burroughs! What are you saying?" Sunny gasps. "Every real estate transaction I've done was based on my sales skills alone. My *talents* never came into it."

"They better not have!" Keith booms. All the adults are laughing now, although my mom looks kind of uncomfortable.

Sienna leans over to me. "Would you go and get me a bucket, please? I think I'm going to spew." I give her a knowing smile.

Sunny's frosted blonde head swivels in its fur collar. "Where are my kids? Sienna? Brody?"

"We're right here," Sienna snaps. "Geez!"

"Oh, there's my precious girl!" Sunny cries, planting a bright pink kiss on her daughter's cheek. Sienna makes a face.

"Okay, let's get you home," Keith says, grabbing his wife's arm. He is this huge, bearlike man, and I've always thought he and Sunny look weird together. She is just so freakishly tiny. Keith turns to my mom. "Thank you for a wonderful dinner, Denise. And thank you for taking pity on us and giving us these leftovers."

"Right," Sunny says, "so now you want me to be Betty frickin' Crocker! I didn't hear any complaints last night when I—"

"All right, all right," my dad interrupts, thank god. "You'd better get home to bed now. See you at the office tomorrow."

We stand on the porch as the Marshalls' minivan backs out of our driveway. I can see my breath in the cold February air as I wave at Sienna, sitting somewhere behind the darkened windows. When the taillights have disappeared, I follow my parents back inside.

My mom makes her way to the kitchen. "He's got his hands full with that one," she chuckles, shaking her head.

My dad follows. "I get a kick out of her," he says, going to the counter and pouring two fingers of scotch into a tumbler. "If I had to lose out on salesperson of the year, I'm glad it was to her."

My mom is busily putting food into the fridge. "Sunny and I have been friends since college, and I love her dearly, but, frankly, I don't know how she does it all. I mean, the career, the children, the marriage...Something's going to suffer, and I just hope it's not the kids."

I could point out here that Sienna and Brody don't appear to be suffering at all. Sure, Brody is weirdly quiet, but he seems perfectly happy. And Sienna is flourishing despite growing up in a household with two working parents who share very permissive views toward the media, fashion, and makeup. In fact, I think her parents' leniency contributes greatly to Sienna's incredible popularity at Red Cedars Secondary. But I don't bother. I already know that my mom is completely unconcerned with my lack of social status. And I'm not in the mood for another lecture on how "developing self-esteem and becoming a strong, self-actualized adult is much more important than winning a popularity / beauty / fashion contest."

My dad takes a sip of his scotch and flips open a real estate magazine. "Well, not every family is lucky enough to have a mom like you. We'd fall apart without you. Isn't that right, kids?"

"Yup," Troy says. He is trying to bounce a tennis ball off his puny bicep and catch it with the same hand. I swear he has ADD, but my parents would rather live in denial than have him tested.

"Yeah," I agree. "Can I have some of that raspberry cheesecake?"

Troy makes an oinking noise. My mom says calmly, "Yes, you may have some cheesecake, Louise. Troy, your sister is not fat. She just has the Burroughs build. Look at your Uncle Leon. He's a very large man."

"Louise is a very large man too," Troy quips, accidentally sending the tennis ball flying toward the dining room wall.

"And you're a scrawny midget!" I yell.

"Enough! Both of you!" my dad bellows. "Troy, put that goddamn tennis ball away and get ready for bed. Louise, eat your cheesecake if you think you need it and get off to bed too."

All the criticism and strife have taken some of the enjoyment out of the long-awaited cheesecake, but it's very good nonetheless. I eat in silence as my mom wipes the counters, keeping a running monologue about how, of course, some outside validation would be nice, but being a homemaker is a legitimate career choice and not to be dismissed like some part-time hobby. My dad is still at the breakfast bar, nursing his scotch and flicking through the magazine.

When I'm finished, I put my plate in the dishwasher. "That was delicious, Mom," I say. "Seriously, it was like a famous chef made it or something."

While I am trying to provide her with some validation for her stay-at-home mom role, she responds with a rather indifferent, "Thanks, honey. Off to bed now."

The next day at school, Sienna finds me at my locker right before lunch. As usual, she is flanked by Jessie Gray and Kimber Bentley. While they don't look particularly alike, there is something similar about the three of them. They're all pretty, stylish, and tiny. Obviously, none of them has a very large Uncle Leon, and if they do, they certainly don't take after him.

"Coming?" Sienna asks.

"Yeah, I'll just grab my lunch," I reply, digging in my locker.

"Ugh," Kimber says, eyeing my burgeoning lunch bag. "I am so not eating today. I was, like, a total pig last night."

Sienna smirks. "What did you have?"

"Only a whole tub of Ben & Jerry's Half Baked."

"Get out! The whole tub?"

Jessie says, "I believe it. Have you seen this girl? She eats ice cream like a mia."

Kimber gasps. "I'm no puker!"

We all laugh, though I can feel my cheeks getting warm. I'm fairly sure that to these three Nicole Richie look-alikes, eating anything more than carrot sticks and diet soda qualifies as binge-eating. Girls their size just don't understand what it takes to sustain a large build like mine.

As I close my locker, our laughter is interrupted by the appearance of Aaron Hansen. Aaron's locker has been beside mine for the past two years—Hansen, Harrison—ever since Mandy Hapwell moved to San Diego. "Hey, Louise," he says, maneuvering his slight frame through us to open his locker.

"Oh...hey, Aaron."

He works at his combination lock. "Are you going to stagecraft after school today?"

I try to ignore the looks exchanged between Jessie and Kimber. Obviously, stagecraft club does not qualify as a cool after-school activity—not like going to the mall or flat-ironing your hair. I clear my throat. "Uh...yeah, maybe."

"You should come," Aaron says, yanking open his lock. "We're blocking scene four of *Rent*."

"Right."

"Ohhh," Jessie says. "Blocking scene four? That sounds way cool."

"Totally," Kimber adds with a malicious giggle.

Aaron reaches into his locker and pulls out his lunch bag. As usual, he's completely unfazed by their catty comments. He looks at me. "See ya later, maybe."

"Maybe," I say with an indifferent shrug. Any show of enthusiasm in front of Kimber and Jessie would be highly uncool.

Aaron walks away, nonchalantly whistling, "Five hundred twenty-five thousand six hundred minutes..."

Watching him go, Jessie says, "Steven Spielberg called. He wants his job back."

Kimber laughs. "I know what you mean. He's so, like..."

"*Serious*," Sienna finishes with a roll of her eyes.

"Yeah. He's so *serious*. Like, what is with that?" Kimber says.

"Hello?" Jessie says. "You're in, like, eleventh grade. You're not going to win an Academy Award for your stupid play." They all laugh.

"A Tony Award," I say.

"What?" Three pairs of eyes turn to me.

"Uh... he's not going to win a *Tony* Award for his stupid play. Academy Awards are for movies and Tony Awards are for plays."

Jessie snorts derisively. "Whatever. He's not going to win anything for a stupid high-school play."

"*Totally*," I agree with a mocking laugh. At least I'm trying to sound mocking, but I'm afraid I just sound lame.

As we walk down the halls to the cafeteria, I wisely keep from expressing any further thoughts on the subject. They would only make fun of me if I told them that I think Aaron Hansen is a really talented director. Besides, Kimber, Jessie, and Sienna are of the opinion that all extracurricular activities are lame. And stagecraft club, in particular, is extra lame. The only reason I'm not ostracized for my attendance is that Sienna supports me honing my artistic abilities on set design. This will only help us when we launch Sienna Lou. But as uncool as it is, I really enjoy painting sets and organizing props. I even think it might be a good career choice, you know... just in case things don't quite take off with the fashion design thing. I wouldn't be my mother's daughter if I didn't have a backup plan.

Seated at our usual table, Kimber cracks open a can of Coke Zero. "So, Audrey's party's going to be awesome."

"I know. I can't wait." Jessie adds, "I've got to get something new to wear."

Sienna says, "Me too. Let's go shopping!"

"I want to lose three pounds first," Jessie says, nibbling a cucumber slice.

With practiced indifference, I bite into my ham and cheese sandwich. My casual air is meant to conceal the fact that this is the first I've heard about the party of the year. While Sienna's popularity has given me a free pass into the in-crowd, times like this just reinforce how tenuous my position really is. I would never be here, at this table, surrounded by the most popular girls at Red Cedars, if not for my friendship with Sienna. Thankfully, our moms have been friends forever and we've practically grown up together. While I can't deny that I'm lucky not to be relegated to one of the loser tables, my exclusion from Audrey's party just reminds me I don't really belong.

But my blasé attitude doesn't fool my best friend. Sienna can read me like a book. "Didn't you get Audrey's text message?"

I shoot her a look. Sienna knows perfectly well I don't have a cell phone. My mom has a number of reasons for banning them, the top three being

1. She doesn't want me to get a brain tumor.

2. She doesn't want me to be distracted by the phone while driving / walking / eating, thus crashing / being run over / choking.

3. Being in constant contact with my friends will nega-

tively influence the bond I have with my parents, leading me to search for positive role models within my peer group, resulting in uninformed and pressured decision-making, not unlike *Lord of the Flies*.

"Oh, right," Sienna says, "the no-phone policy. Well, that's why you haven't heard about it. Audrey sent everyone a text. But you're totally coming! We'll go together."

I give her a small smile and my heart surges with gratitude. With Sienna around, I never feel left out for long.

As if on cue, our future hostess approaches the table, a nearly ubiquitous lollipop held in her manicured hand. "Ladies," Audrey says, taking a seat next to Kimber, "can you tell me—what comes before Part B?"

"Partaaay!" my three companions cry in unison. Luckily, they drown out my questioning "Part A?"

"We were just talking about it," Sienna says, taking a bite of her carrot stick.

"It's going to be sooo fun," Kimber gushes. "I don't think I can wait three whole weeks."

"You'll have to," Audrey says. "My parents aren't going away until then." She puts the lollipop in her mouth rather suggestively. "Besides, I'm not having a party until I get my highlights done."

I look at her auburn hair. I'd never noticed before, but there are definitely some copper tones there.

"I want to get highlights too," Sienna says, although her hair is already made up of several shades of blonde: honey, caramel, and wheat. I swear every strand of my hair is the same mousy brown.

"But your hair's so gorgeous already!" Kimber says.

"I know!" Jessie agrees. "I totally hate you!"

Everyone laughs, but then Audrey wisely counsels. "It'll have a lot more body once you get it done."

"Yeah, I just have to ask my mom if she'll shell out two hundred bucks for it," Sienna replies.

For the second time in three minutes I feel out of my element. Whenever Sienna and her cohorts talk about beauty, fashion, or dieting, my contributions are few and far between. It's not that I don't care about my looks; I'm just not *consumed* by them. I could blame my mother for this. You can't be constantly bombarded with female empowerment messages without some of them sinking in. But more likely it's because I'm not really in the same league as these girls in the looks department. It's not like I'm a complete ogre, but all four of them are utterly gorgeous. Okay, Kimber isn't quite as pretty as the rest of them, but she makes up for it by spending hours flat-ironing her pale blonde hair. But since I will one day be one-half of the straight female version of Dolce & Gabbana, I should probably make more of an effort.

"I'm going to ask my mom about getting highlights too," I say.

There is a moment of surprised silence, broken by Audrey. "That's good, Louise." There is something slightly condescending in her tone. Or maybe I'm just being paranoid.

"It would brighten up your face, for sure," Kimber adds.

Sienna nods. "It would."

"And while you're at it," Jessie contributes, "you should get some layers around your face."

"It definitely needs some shaping," Audrey says, picking up a dull strand of my shapeless hair.

Kimber furrows her brow. "I'd normally recommend a flat iron, but with the shape of her face, I think she needs more body."

"There're always hot rollers," Jessie says.

The conversation continues in this manner for the entirety of the lunch hour. Really, they have all become quite passionate about my hair makeover. I know I should feel flattered. I've never had this much attention from Sienna's friends. But while their comments are all well-intentioned and constructive, they're making me feel even more insecure about my looks. By the time the bell rings, I realize that if my parents won't pay for some highlights and shaping, I will have to commit suicide! Either that or join a convent, where my hair will be safely covered by one of those nun hats.

As we head to our next class, Sienna walks beside me. "Good for you," she says. "I'm glad you're making more of an effort with your hair and stuff."

"Oh...well..." I laugh awkwardly, unsure how to respond.

She gives my arm a squeeze. "See you after school."

I wouldn't say I *stewed* about the state of my hair for the entire weekend, but it was definitely on my mind. Everywhere I looked, I saw highlights, lowlights, and layers—from the video store clerk to the middle-aged woman who served us at Boston Pizza. But when I went to stagecraft club after school today and noticed that several of the so-called drama nerds had nicer hair than I did, it was the last straw. As soon as I got home, I went to my mom, who was making dinner in the kitchen.

"My hair *desperately* needs some highlights and shaping."

She cocks an eyebrow, amused. "Desperately?"

"It's true!" I say, going to the fridge to search for a snack. "It's limp and drab and doesn't have enough body for the shape of my face."

My mom stops chopping carrots and looks at me. "You're a beautiful girl and you have beautiful hair. Who's putting these ideas in your head?"

I rip the top off a Jell-O pudding cup and say, "No one. It's just that everyone's hair looks way better than mine."

"That's not true."

"It is true!"

"Like whose?"

"Sienna, Audrey, Kimber, Jessie."

"I don't think Jessie's hair is all that fantastic," my mom says, resuming her chopping.

"Oh, okay. Everyone else's hair is better except Jessie's. See? You agree with me."

She turns to face me, knife in hand. "What's this really about?"

"My hair. It needs highlights and shaping."

"How many times have we discussed not trying to look like the girls in magazines? Those supermodels don't look like that when they get up in the morning, you know."

"I know, I know. And they all have eating disorders and drug problems." I roll my eyes.

"That's right." Suddenly, my mom gets a twinkle in her eye. "I think I know what this is really about. Is there a boy you're interested in?"

"MOM!" God, she is so embarrassing. Despite the fact that we're alone in the house, I can feel my cheeks turning red. I mean, what does she think I am? Twelve? It's not normal to be having this conversation for the first time eight months before my seventeenth birthday. I'm sure Sunny talked to Sienna about boys five years ago!

Unfortunately, my mom takes my embarrassment as an admission. "What's his name?" she prods, looking positively gleeful.

"There's no one," I snap, "probably because my hair is so hideous."

"Honey," she says, and I know what's coming, "if a boy only likes you because you have nice hair, that's not really much of a relationship, is it? You have so many other great qualities: you're smart, you're funny, you're tall..."

"No boy's even going to look at me with this hair," I grouch.

"Your dad fell in love with the person inside me," she continues, tapping her chest. "It wasn't about my hair or my body or my breasts..."

God! Make her stop!

"And that's why our love has endured, through pregnancies and weight gain, good times and bad."

"Yeah, I get it," I say, "but I don't think there's anything wrong with wanting to look your best. It will boost my self-confidence and make me more outgoing."

She returns her attention to the carrots. "How much do highlights cost?"

"Well... Audrey goes to this really great salon and there are really nice people there and they do a really great job and the highlights last a super long time—like, six months."

"How much?"

"Two hundred."

My mom bursts into laughter like this is the funniest thing she's ever heard. Really, she is so out of touch. She lives in some weird, ancient reality where men fall in love with the person inside and you never need to spend more than nineteen dollars at Magicuts on your hair. "It's not that much," I grumble.

"Right!" she laughs. "Try telling that to your father."

"I'm sure Sunny will pay for Sienna's highlights."

"Well, that's Sunny's prerogative, but in our household we watch our spending, and there's no way on god's green earth that I'm going to pay two hundred bucks for you to dye your hair."

I bite my tongue before I say something spiteful like, *You're just lucky you met Dad in the olden days when guys weren't so picky.*

As I'm about to stomp off in a pout, my mom says, "Maybe you should consider getting an after-school job?"

"Are you serious?"

"I worked when I was your age," she says, scooping a handful of chopped carrots into a large metal pot.

"I have a job. It's called school."

"It's really nice to have your own money," my mom says. "You can spend it on anything you want—even highlights."

"Yeah, but I'm already so busy..." But I trail off to consider the suggestion. Having my own money would open a whole new world to me, a world of shapely, highlighted hair that could lead to increased popularity and possibly even boyfriends.

"And it's great to have an after-school job on your résumé," my mom continues. "It'll show that you're a responsible girl on your college applications..."

That's true. And if I got a job at a clothing retailer, it could even help my fashion design career. Of course, Sienna is the fashionista in our partnership, but it wouldn't hurt for me to brush up on some of the basics. I'm sold! It's the answer to all my hair problems. Now, I'll just have to concoct a résumé of my nonexistent work experience and I can start applying. "That's a great idea, Mom." I kiss her cheek. "I'm going to start on my résumé right away."

"That's the independent young woman I'm raising," she says, giving me a wink. "But I'm really going to need your help this week. It's your dad's fortieth birthday party on Saturday."

"Well, I'll be kind of busy looking for a job..."

"We're all going to have to pitch in," she says in a tone not open for debate. "I've got so much to do before Saturday. Troy needs new soccer cleats, and I've got to pick up the food, prepare it, buy all the decorations..."

"Okay," I say, mentally adding freelance catering and event planning to my résumé.

"I'll need to get the liquor, and sort out some kind of music..."

Bartender and DJ.

"...and all of this without your dad catching on. Although, with the hours he's been keeping lately, I don't think we have to worry. By the time he gets home from work, he's so exhausted, I'm sure we could set up a ten-piece orchestra in the living room and he'd walk right by."

"Okay." I give in. I guess I can live with the drab, limp hideousness of my hair for a little while longer.

"Thanks, sweetie," she says. "Can you set the table for three? Your dad won't be here for dinner. He's got to take some papers over to a buyer tonight."

My mom, my brother, and I have just tucked into our meal of homemade chicken stew and whole-wheat focaccia bread when we hear the whir of the garage door opening. "Oh!" my mom says, sounding pleased. "Your dad made it home after all." She moves to meet him at the door and then turns back to us. "Ixnay on the artypay."

"What?" Troy asks, confused.

I look at him. "You're kidding, right?"

"No!" he snaps. "I don't speak French!"

"Oh my god!" I cry, nearly helpless with laughter. "It's pig latin, you dork!"

"*You're* the pig!" he yells at me.

At this precise moment, my parents enter the room. "Well, isn't this nice," my dad says sarcastically. "I finally get to have dinner with my family and this is what I walk in on."

My mom says, "Troy, enough with the name calling."

"Yeah," I yell at him. "I'm probably going to get an eating disorder because of you!"

"Good!" Troy says and then under his breath, "Maybe you'll die from it."

"What's that, Troy?" I say loudly. "You hope I *die* from an eating disorder? Well, that is really sweet."

My mom whirls on him. "That's a horrible thing to say! Apologize right now."

This is the point when my dad loses his temper. Maybe it's because he's not around us as much, but he seems to find our harmless sibling bickering unbearable. "That's enough!" he booms. "Troy, go to your room until you're ready to apologize to your sister."

My brother jumps out of his chair, nearly upending it. As he storms out of the dining room, he mutters quietly, "Fat bitch."

"Did you hear that?" I ask. "Did anyone hear that?"

"You can go to your room too," my dad grumbles, walking to the counter and placing his briefcase on it.

"Why? What did I do?"

"I just need some peace and quiet," he says, closing his eyes and massaging his temples.

"Let me make you a drink," my mom says, kneading his shoulders. "Louise, take your stew into the other room."

When I'm done eating, I take the cordless phone to my room and call Sienna. "Did you ask your mom about your hair?" I ask. "What did she say?"

"She said she'll think about it, which basically means yes. I mean, it's not like she doesn't spend a fortune on her own hair. And I think she's feeling guilty because she's been working so much lately."

"That's great," I say. While I'm sincerely happy for Sienna, I can't help feeling a slight twinge of envy. Everything just seems to come so easy for her. Of course, Sunny Lewis-Marshall would never think to make her only daughter toil like a slave to pay for highlights. Sunny obviously gets what it takes to be popular these days. Or maybe she's just too busy selling real estate to teach her daughter about boys liking you for your sense of humor and personality instead of your looks. It's just my luck to have a mother who's chosen to make her children her life's work.

Sometimes it amazes me that my mom and Sunny are best friends. They're just so different. Sunny is all about real estate and fitted skirt suits and chemical peels. My mom is all about feminism and keeping your maiden name and hairy armpits. Okay, she doesn't take it that far, but compared to Sunny, she's practically a hippie! They're an odd pair, but I guess when you've been friends as long as they have, differences don't matter. It's not like Sienna and I are exactly twins, and I know *we*'ll be best friends forever.

Before I can tell her about my mother's excellent plan to have me earn the money for highlights by devoting all my free time to some minimum-wage job at the mall, Sienna says, "I've got to go. My mom's going out, and I need to ask her if I can use her car tomorrow."

When I return the phone to the kitchen, I search for my parents. I plan to guilt-trip them by relaying the fact that Sunny's going to fork over the money for Sienna to enhance her already beautiful hair. While my mom won't fall for it, my dad is a little less savvy and could maybe be convinced. But I find my mom and Troy in the living room, watching a rerun of *The Simpsons*.

"Where's Dad?"

She looks up at me. "Oh, there was an emergency at one of his spec homes. A pipe burst or something."

"That's a drag," I say.

"Yeah." She pats the couch beside her. "Come watch TV with us."

Settling in next to her, I stare at the bratty antics of Bart Simpson. While I question my mom's judgment in letting my disturbed brother watch a show so brimming with ideas to get him into trouble, I no longer resent her suggestion for an after-school job. Even if her parenting is a little too hands-on, I know she means well.

The week is a flurry of school, stagecraft (*Rent* is going to be so awesome!), and birthday party preparations. Somehow, I manage to hide myself away in my dad's basement home office for a few hours. In that time, I fabricate—I mean, *create*—a fairly impressive résumé. The objective line alone should be enough to get me hired.

Objective: To contribute to the success of your company through my hard work, enthusiasm, creativity, and excellent manners while gaining valuable work experience to help me reach my higher education and long-term career goals.

The résumé-building website I checked out said to keep your objective to one line, but that's simply not possible for someone with as much to offer as I have.

On Saturday morning, I take my mom's car to Willowbrook Mall. The only reason I'm allowed to escape on "surprise party day" is that my mom has given me a list of last-minute errands to run for her in between submitting job applications. Brimming with confidence, I enter the rather dated shopping center. I'm wearing black pants, a cropped, beige blazer, and a colorful scarf. This exact outfit (or a more expensive designer version) was featured in *ELLEgirl* magazine. Apparently, this outfit says hip and stylish without going overboard into trendy, fashion-junkie territory. The magazine assures me that most employers prefer a conservative look, conveying responsibility, trustworthiness, and a lower probability of showing up at work hungover.

When I have delivered résumés to virtually every clothing retailer (except Selena's, which everyone knows is a grandma store) and most of the outlets in the food court, I tackle the list of chores my mom gave me.

Two hours later I arrive home, weighed down with bags full of party supplies and snack food. "Thank god!" my mom says, like I've been missing for weeks. "Let's get that food into the fridge and put the banner up on the feature wall. Troy!" she calls at the top of her lungs. My hyperactive brother pitches himself off the top stair, hurtling his puny body into the kitchen. "Carry those cases of beer and wine into the garage. Louise, go put the hand towels out in the guest bathroom." I start to move in that direction. "What are you doing?" my mom snaps. "I asked you to put the food away and the banner up! Will you listen, please?"

Thank god the party starts in a few hours. I'm afraid my mom might collapse under the stress of all this covert event planning.

The guests begin to arrive at 4:30 p.m. Sunny, Sienna, and Brody are the first (Keith has had my dad at the driving range since 10:00 a.m., and then they went to shop for a digital camera Keith was interested in). Sunny is carrying an enormous bunch of helium-filled balloons with "Life begins at 40" written on them. "Louise, would you tie these to one of the dining room chairs?" she asks me as she shrugs out of her rabbit-fur coat.

"Sure."

"You're a doll. Now," she says, clapping her manicured hands together, "put me to work, Denise. What can I do to help?"

Sienna follows me to the dining room, where I attempt to anchor the balloon bouquet. "Let's go to your room."

But before I can respond, my mother cries, "Louise! Ice!" and I'm sent to the deep freeze in the garage to collect a bag of ice cubes. When Sienna tries to tag along, Sunny intervenes. "Make yourself useful, Sienna. That tray of cold cuts needs to be put out, and you can put those chips and pretzels into bowls."

People continue to stream into the house for the next twenty minutes. Finally, at 4:55 p.m., Sunny's cell phone rings. This is the cue that Keith and my dad are just minutes away. "No, I don't need you to pick anything up for dinner," she says, winking at the assembled guests. "We'll see you soon, hon."

"Okay, everyone!" my mom cries to the fifty or so people milling about the living room and kitchen. "Find somewhere to hide. They'll be here any minute."

When everyone yells "Surprise!" it's obvious from my dad's expression that he had no idea. He actually tears up a little as he hugs my mom. "When did you do all this?" he says, taking in the crepe paper streamers and the "Lordy, lordy, look who's forty" banner I've tacked up.

"Happy birthday, Dad," I say, elbowing my way through the crowd to give him a hug.

He kisses the top of my head. "Thanks, sweetheart. And thanks for helping your mom with all this."

Suddenly Sienna is tugging at my sleeve. "Let's go to your room."

"Sure." And leaving the adults to their festivities, we sneak away.

When we are safe behind closed doors, Sienna flops on my bed. "I can't bear to watch my mom get all drunk and flirty again. It's, like, so sad."

"I know," I say to commiserate, although thankfully my mother does not get drunk and flirty.

Sienna changes the subject. "What are you going to wear to Audrey's party?"

I perch on the corner of my bed. "I don't know yet. What are you going to wear?" While I'm not completely without personal style (thanks to *ELLEgirl*), I don't have Sienna's natural flair for fashion. Really, the girl has a gift. She can throw on long beads or a leather belt and look both retro and hip. When I've tried to mimic her approach, I end up looking like a refugee from a 1970s punk band. Sienna knows what's cool before it's even cool.

"We should go shopping," she says. "I want to get something really cute. There're going to be lots of hot guys there."

"Yeah?" I am interested. "Like who?"

"Daniel Noran, Jake Lawrence, and those guys."

"Oh." My voice conveys my disappointment.

"Oh right," Sienna teases, "they're not your *type*."

"Shut up," I say, slapping at her playfully. But she's right. I've never gone for those good-looking, popular guys who wear designer polo shirts and drive sports cars. Since these guys don't go for me either, this has worked out quite well so far.

Sienna continues, "What *is* your type anyway?"

Chewing on my bottom lip, I ponder this question. I don't exactly know, but I'd like a guy who is artistic, passionate, and intelligent, with a dark sense of humor and an appreciation for theater, film, and music. Unfortunately, there seems to be a serious shortage of this type in Langley. The only one who even comes close is Aaron Hansen, but given the fact that he is possibly even punier than my brother, dating him would be physically impossible. And of course I could never admit, even to Sienna, that the king of the drama nerds comes closest to my ideal guy!

Finally, I answer. "Well, I don't really know, but I'm sure I'll find him when we move to New York. There'll be lots of—"

Suddenly, my door flies open and there stands my brother. "Get lost, you freak!" I scream before he even has time to open his mouth.

"Mom needs you downstairs!" he yells back angrily.

"Okay. Get out."

"Fat bitch!" The door slams behind him.

"I guess we'd better go help out."

Sienna drags herself off the bed. "Yeah, I guess."

My mom makes a beeline for me the moment I enter the kitchen. "Oh, there you are! Take this wine," she says, handing me an open bottle of red, "and make sure everyone's drinks are filled. Sienna, you can take the white."

As I make my way through the crowded house refilling glasses, it really doesn't seem like anyone needs more booze. Most of the guests are talking way too loudly and making inappropriate jokes, a sure sign they are well on their way to drunksville. But I play the dutiful daughter, smiling at my dad's friends as they marvel at the fact that I am looking so grown-up and compliment me on my helpfulness.

An hour or so later, my mom is at my side. "We're going to have the cake now," she says breathlessly. "Round everyone up and bring them into the dining room. Where is your dad? Go find him, Louise."

"Do you want me to round people up or go find dad?" She shoots me a look that says I'd better work on my multitasking.

"Troy!" she calls for my brother, who is inhaling Doritos with Brody. "Go downstairs into your dad's office and get the cake. It's sitting on the filing cabinet."

"Okay." He starts to bound away.

"And be careful with it!" she calls after him.

Wandering through the house, I inform our guests about the upcoming festivities. "We're going to sing 'Happy Birthday' and have the cake now," I say. "Has anyone seen my dad?" Finally, I head outside to the back deck, where a handful of smokers have congregated. My dad isn't among them—not surprisingly, since he doesn't smoke, but I thought he might be chatting with Keith, who is what he calls a *social smoker*. "We're going to have the cake now," I say.

"Okay, fun's over," Keith jokes, butting out his cigar on the railing. "Back inside, everyone."

Returning to the dining room I notice that only a few people have actually heeded my call for cake. My mom is beginning to look a little concerned that her well-orchestrated event may not proceed as planned. "Where is Troy with the cake?" she says to no one in particular. "Louise, did you find your dad?"

I'm about to respond that Dad is MIA when Troy suddenly bursts into the room from the basement stairwell. The first thing I notice is that he is cake-less. Before I can comment on his short attention span and inability to focus on simple instructions, I notice the look on his face. Never before have I seen such horror on my brother's features. My mom catches it too and instantly says, "Troy, what's wrong?"

But Troy doesn't stop to explain. He runs through the living room and out the front door into the frigid night.

What happens next is almost too hard to believe. It's like some prime-time dramedy, except it is too sick and twisted for television. Okay, maybe it could run on HBO, but there's no way my mom would let me watch it. My mother is obviously concerned. Not only has my brother forgotten the birthday cake, but he's run out into the cold February evening wearing nothing but a T-shirt. "What the heck?..." she mumbles as she hurries toward the front door. She's only gone a few steps when my dad suddenly appears from the basement.

"Troy!" he calls, looking around frantically. "Where's Troy?"

"He just ran out the front door like a bat out of hell," my mom says. "What's going on with that kid? He's going to catch his death if he doesn't get back in here soon."

My dad doesn't respond but runs to the front porch. "Troy!" he calls. "Come back, son. Please, come back!" I follow my parents, also wondering what is up with my brother. But then, nothing Troy does really surprises me. In fact, I almost feel a little smug. I've been telling my parents for years that Troy has serious, undiagnosed mental problems, and his current actions just seem to confirm it. The panic in my dad's voice is a little alarming though. And it is this tone that has drawn a number of party guests to gather around the front door, murmuring with concern.

"I'm going after him," my dad finally says, coming back inside and heading to the closet for his coat.

"I'll go, Len," my mom says. "It's your birthday. You stay here. Louise, go get the cake."

As I turn to head to the basement, I see Sunny Lewis-Marshall lingering at the back of the crowd. Her face is pale and tears are streaming untouched down her face. My mom notices her too. "Sunny?" she asks, going to her. "What's wrong?"

"Oh god, Denise," Sunny moans.

"Sunny..." my dad begins, something almost threatening in his voice.

My mom looks to him and then back at her weeping friend. "Will someone please tell me what the hell is going on here?"

"Denise...oh god, I'm so sorry." Sunny sags a little as she grasps my mom's hands.

"Stop it, Sunny," my dad commands. "Not here. Not now."

"For god's sake, Len," my mom snaps. "Someone had better tell me what sent my son running out of the house right now or I'm going to lose it!"

"I'd like to know too." Keith Marshall's hulking form has materialized.

Suddenly, Sunny collapses to the floor. "It—It just happened!" she wails, clutching at her husband's shins.

"I didn't mean for it to happen! We were wrong! We were so wrong!"

I am still trying to piece together what she's talking about when Keith punches my dad in the face. As I mentioned, Keith is what you'd call burly, while my dad is more sinewy. My dad staggers backward, crashing into our next-door neighbors, the Van Leusdens. (I can tell by their horrified expressions that they won't be asking a girl from such an unstable home to cat-sit for them again.) Blood begins to pour from my dad's nose, spurting dramatically all over Mrs. Van Leusden's blouse. She lets out a high-pitched shriek of horror, as does my mom. Keith turns his attentions to the crumpled form at his feet. "You bitch! How could you?"

Everything seems to move in fast motion after that. The general consensus is that my dad needs to go to the hospital, and apparently, so does Keith (he thinks he might have broken a finger on my dad's cheekbone). As the four of them jostle out the door, still crying and bickering, my parents manage to find time to turn to me and say, "Find your brother, Louise. If he freezes to death, we'll blame you." Okay, maybe they didn't say those exact words, but that is the gist of it.

Lucky for me, Troy is not far away. When he saw the party guests making a mass exodus from our home, he returned through the sliding patio doors. Soon, the only occupants in the deserted living room are my brother and me, and Sienna and Brody. "God," I say, fumbling for words in the awkward silence, "major drama."

Surprisingly, Brody is the one who responds. "Weird..." is all he says.

After a long pause, Sienna says, "We're gonna get going." Although her dad's minivan is still parked at the curb, he hadn't thought to leave the keys. Sienna dials her cell. A few minutes later, Audrey shows up in the driveway in her mom's Volkswagen. With a brief "See ya later," Sienna and Brody make their exit.

So now I am sitting facing my brother across a table strewn with empty wineglasses, half-eaten dips, and bowls of chip crumbs. While Troy and I rarely have a discourse that doesn't revolve around being too fat or too skinny, deep down I can admit that he is my brother and I therefore harbor some loving, familial feelings toward him. "Are you okay?" I ask.

"I guess."

"Do you want a Coke? Or some chips or something?"

Troy makes a face. "I don't think I'll ever be able to eat again."

I restrain myself from cracking a joke about him disappearing into thin air. "What did you see downstairs?"

"You don't want to know."

I don't, but I sort of do. "Just tell me," I say. "I'm in eleventh grade. I can handle it."

He looks up at me and his eyes are shining with unshed tears. "I walked into Dad's office and I saw him standing there. I thought he was upset at first, his face was all twisted and weird. And then I saw Sunny. She was kneeling in front of him and...I think she was—"

"STOP!" I say. My skin has begun to crawl like I am covered in ants. I stand and begin to scratch myself frantically. "God, why are you telling me that? That's sick!"

"I know it's sick!" Troy snaps. "You said you wanted to know."

He's right. I had said I wanted to know. But I really thought I would handle whatever he had to tell better than this. I'm almost seventeen! I hang around with a fairly sexually experienced group of girls. I mean, I know for a fact that Jessie and Audrey have both given and received head. And Kimber actually considers herself quite gifted in the oral sex department. Sienna and I are really the only holdouts. So while my personal experience is nil, I've developed a fairly laid-back attitude toward blow jobs and such over the last couple of years. But this is entirely different! How can you be expected to be laid-back when the blow job in question involves your dad and your best friend's mom?

But I suddenly remember that I'm the mature one here. I need to pull myself together. "I'm really sorry you had to see that," I say.

"Too bad you didn't see it instead of me," Troy says quietly.

"Why?"

"Because I'm never going to eat again."

Despite the gravity of the situation, he's still an idiot. "Oh, shut up. Think about what this means for Mom and Dad."

"Do you think they'll get divorced?"

"I don't know. They might. But you never know. Maybe they have a more *untraditional* kind of relationship. I saw this thing on *The Tyra Banks Show* and it said a lot more people are swingers these days."

"You think Mom and Dad and Keith and Sunny are *swingers*?" Troy looks like this revelation might cause him to dive off the nearest bridge.

"Well...I doubt Mom would be into that..."

"It wouldn't really work then, would it?"

"True."

"And why would Keith have punched Dad if this was just normal Saturday-night behavior?"

I don't like how Troy is suddenly sounding like the wise one here. "Uh, Troy," I say, "I think I know a little bit more about sex and relationships than you do, since I actually have several friends who *have* sex and relationships—" But my diatribe is cut short by a sudden noise. My brother and I stare at each other as we hear the whir of the garage door opening and a car pulling in.

Eventually, my mom makes her way into the dining room, alone. From the look on her face, it's evident she is not a swinger and this was not just normal Saturday-night swapsies. Her eyes are red-rimmed and her face splotchy. Without a word, she pulls out a chair and sits next to me.

"Kids, there's no easy way to tell you this so I'm just going to lay it on the line. I hope you're both mature enough to handle what I'm about to say." She clears her throat. "Apparently, your father and *Mrs. Lewis-Marshall*..." My stomach drops uncomfortably. We have never called Sunny *Mrs. Lewis-Marshall*, and the words have a certain finality to them. I can see my mom's point though. I guess when someone blows your husband at the surprise birthday party you planned for him, you feel on less friendly terms.

"...have been having a...physical relationship. Your father won't be living here anymore. I'm sorry."

"Oh god," I say, starting to cry.

Troy jumps up. "Fucking bastard!" he punches the wall. Luckily, his puny arm has little impact on the drywall.

"Troy! Language!" my mom cries angrily. "Just because your father has deserted us, this family is not going to dissolve into anarchy. You two need to be strong. I—" Her voice cracks. "I need you to be strong."

I go to my mom and hug her. We hold each other, sobbing for what feels like an hour. Part of me feels like I'm too old to be blubbering like a baby about this, but another part of me is just so incredibly sad. When the feeling of our tear-slicked cheeks rubbing together is getting a little uncomfortable, my mom takes a deep breath. She pulls away from the hug and wipes at her face.

"Look at this mess," she says, surveying the aftermath of the party. "I'd better get busy."

"I'll do it," I say, looking at her drawn face. Of course this is hard on me, but it's even harder on my mom. Not only has her husband left her, but she's been betrayed by her best friend too. I only have to deal with the fact that my dad, whom I have always loved and adored, is a cheating scumbag.

My mom looks up at me and the gratitude in her eyes tells me I've chosen the right course. "Oh, honey," she says, her voice quivering. "Thank you for being so strong. What would I do without you?"

"Get some rest," I say, giving her another quick hug.

Alone in the kitchen, I begin to remove all remnants of my dad's birthday party. Normally, I'm fairly environmentally conscious, but nothing is recycled tonight. I chuck out the paper banners, the beer bottles, the chips and leftover dips. I slit the balloons with a knife, letting the helium quietly seep out of them so as not to wake my mom. Normally, Troy and I would have breathed it in and made funny voices, but he's locked in his room probably having some kind of psychological meltdown, and I'm not in the mood. Finally, when three large garbage bags in the back alley are the only evidence that Len Harrison turned forty today, I head to bed. Alone, in my dark bedroom, I clutch my stuffed unicorn and cry myself to sleep.

The next morning, my dad calls the house around ten. My brother answers. "You fucking bastard!" he says, dropping the receiver like it was scorching his hand.

"Troy!" my mom yells from her prone position on the couch. "Language!"

Picking up the cordless phone, I take it to my mom. I give her a supportive, hopeful smile. "You can do this," my hopeful smile says. "It was just a birthday blow job. There's no need to throw away eighteen years of marriage over it." She takes the receiver. "Hello?" she says.

I retreat to the kitchen but linger just around the corner trying to eavesdrop. Apparently, my dad is doing most of the talking, as my mom is basically mute except for the odd "Give me a break" and "Oh, come off it, Len." Finally she says, "I don't know if the children want to see you. They're feeling pretty humiliated and betrayed . . . Okay . . . Okay . . . Well, we'll discuss that when you get here."

My heart lurches in my chest. My dad is coming here? Now? I hadn't realized it before, but I'm not ready to see him. Does he think he can just do it with my best friend's mom and then waltz in here and take us out for ice cream?

I don't freakin' think so! I will refuse to see him, and I'm sure Troy will do the same. We'll make him pay for what he's done. We'll wear him down until he finally comes home, crying and begging for forgiveness, tearfully promising to have himself chemically castrated so that he never humiliates us like that again.

But the next thing I know, my mom has washed her face and thrown a cardigan over her new and highly unflattering sweatpants and flannel shirt ensemble. "Your father and I are going for a drive. We have a lot to figure out," she says absently as she wanders through the house looking for her purse. "If I'm not home by lunch, make sure your brother eats something."

"Okay."

I hear the sound of my father's Infiniti pulling into the driveway. I retreat farther into the kitchen, not wanting him to see me through the front window. I'm momentarily afraid that Troy will fly out the door and launch himself onto dad's windshield, swearing and pounding at the glass in some ADD-fueled rage, but he stays holed up in his room. Purse found, my mom hurries out the door.

She is definitely not home in time for lunch. And as the winter sky begins to darken, I'm afraid she might not make it home for dinner. I knock on Troy's door.

"It's getting late. Do you want a sandwich or something?"

"I'm not hungry," he grumbles.

I go in and sit on the edge of his bed. Troy is lying on his stomach, picking at a seam in his wallpaper. "I'm not hungry either," I say, before I realize I've just given him an opening for a fat joke. But surprisingly, my brother doesn't say the expected "That's a first." He just keeps picking at the blue paper.

"What do you think Mom and Dad are talking about?" I ask. Troy just shrugs, so I continue. "Of course, I don't want them to get a divorce, but I don't know how Mom could ever forgive him. I mean, Sunny Lewis-Marshall was her best friend, and who knows how long she's been doing it with Dad."

Troy rolls over. "I don't want to fucking talk about it, okay?"

"Okay, okay," I say, leaving before he has another wall-punching episode. The kid needed therapy before all this happened, but now he might have to be committed.

I decide to call Sienna. If anyone can relate to what I'm going through, it's her. I bet her parents are also off on a drive right now, leaving their children to fend for themselves as they discuss the future. Dialing her number, I listen to it ring in Sienna's house. Suddenly, a thought strikes me. What if Keith and Sunny are not off on a drive? What if, unlike my parents, they actually want to include their children in the decision-making process and they're having some kind of family meeting right now? What if Sunny—or should I say *Mrs. Lewis-Marshall*—answers? Yuck! I don't want to talk to that...*father-blower*! I hang up the phone. I'll call Sienna on her cell.

I've just started to dial when I hear my mom returning. Troy bursts out of his room and we both rush to the door to meet her.

"So?" I ask as soon as she walks in. "What's going on?"

Troy is at my shoulder. "What did that bastard say?"

My mom sighs heavily and momentarily closes her eyes. She looks exhausted, like she could fall asleep standing right there in the mud room. Frankly, she wasn't looking all that hot when she left, but it's obvious she's been through the wringer. If ever there was a time for her to revisit her anti-makeup stance, this is it.

"Look," she says finally, opening her eyes, "we haven't made any final decisions, but I don't want you to worry. Your father and I will make sure you're both well taken care of, even if he's off living in some love nest with Mrs. Lewis-Marshall."

"That *prick*!" Troy screams, doing some kind of flying martial arts kick in the air.

"Mom, I think Troy needs a sedative or something."

"Louise . . . I just want to lie down." She walks past us and heads to her room. Just before she goes through the door she says, "There's money in my wallet if you want to order a pizza."

❀

While I would have thought that the current state of my parents' marriage would be ample cause for a day off school, apparently that's not the case. At 7:00 a.m. my mom shuffles into my bedroom in her robe, flicking on the light. "Get up, Louise. You're going to be late."

"What?" I grumble blearily. "You expect me to go to school today?"

"Your education is not going to suffer just because your father can't keep it in his pants. I'll make you some toast." She shuffles off to the kitchen.

I'm even more annoyed when I get to school and realize that Sienna is not in attendance. Apparently the Marshalls have no policy regarding the importance of a high school education when your mother has recently revealed herself to be a nymphomaniac. "Hi, Jessie," I say when I pass her in the hallway between classes.

"Oh, hey, Louise. Is Sienna sick? She wasn't in chem."

"Yeah, she's sick," I say, moving on before I'm asked to elaborate. It's not a lie. If Sienna feels anywhere near as bad as I do when I think about what happened at my dad's birthday party, she has every right to be absent. At lunch, I throw myself into set design for *Rent*. Opening night is still a couple of months away, but there is a ton of work to do. Besides, without Sienna there, I don't feel comfortable hanging out with the other girls.

For the entire week I work on sets at lunch hour. On Friday, Sienna has still not returned to school. "She must be really sick," Audrey comments to me in our history class. "I phoned her last night, but nobody answered."

I clear my throat nervously. "There's a nasty virus going around. Her whole family's got it."

"Well, if you talk to her, tell her I'll come visit her if she wants some company. I drink this organic echinacea tea, and I never catch colds."

But, of course, I won't be talking to Sienna. I've called her cell phone every day, but she must have it turned off. I guess she doesn't want to talk to anyone as she deals with the fallout from the birthday-party blow job. And there's no way I'm calling her home number.

Over the next few days, my parents speak sporadically on

the phone, but the conversations usually result in my mom slamming the receiver down, then hurrying to her bedroom, where she puts Carly Simon on the CD player and sobs into her pillow. While I do mourn the loss of the perfect family we'd so long taken for granted, I'm too angry at my dad to feel much sadness.

Then on Sunday morning, things finally come to a head. My mom wanders into the kitchen in her now ever-present sweatpants and slippers. "Your dad's coming by to talk to you in ten minutes."

Troy, who is seated at the breakfast bar, half stands. He looks about to launch into another fit, but the withering looks he receives from us halt him in his tracks. I speak on his behalf. "What if we don't want to talk to him?"

My mom sighs. "He's still your father, even if he is in the throes of a severe midlife crisis he won't admit to." She pours herself a cup of coffee. "Besides, I think it's important you hear what he's got to say for himself."

I am sick with nerves as I wait for Dad's arrival. The fact that my mom has returned to her bed does not signal a happy family reunion. I wonder where he's been staying? A hotel? A youth hostel? Ha! He's hardly a youth. Maybe he's been living in the Infiniti? To distract myself, I clean the kitchen while Troy glumly continues eating his cereal.

Right on time, his car pulls into the driveway. I look at my brother. "Try to control yourself," I say. "Spazzing out isn't going to help anything."

Strangely, my dad lets himself into the house as if he still lives here or something. "Kids?" he calls, with a surprisingly jovial tone in his voice.

"We're in here," I call back, my voice sounding tense and strained.

"Hi, guys!" he says brightly. I have to admit, he looks good. A slight bruise on the bridge of his nose is the only evidence of last week's fight with Keith. He even looks a little tanned. God, has he been going to a tanning salon? My mom's right. He *is* having a midlife crisis! He looks around. "Is your mom here?"

"She's in bed," Troy snaps.

"She spends a lot of time there lately," I add.

My dad chooses to ignore our comments as he helps himself to a cup of coffee. "Let's sit down," he says, going to the dining room. My brother and I follow.

My dad takes a seat and clears his throat, as if he's preparing to close the deal on a house he's selling. "First off, let me apologize for what happened at my birthday party. That couldn't have been easy for you—especially you, son."

Troy mumbles something incoherent with a definite *f* sound.

"But, everything happens for a reason, and in retrospect, I think that it was fate."

"Right," I snort.

My dad looks at me. "Louise, we could do without your attitude at a time like this."

My attitude? My attitude? You cruise in here with your fake tan and your nouveau spiritualism and you expect to get away with it? But I don't say this out loud. Instead, I give him a piercing look and slouch farther down in my seat.

"In fact," my dad continues, clearing his throat again, "I'm actually glad it happened." Somehow, Troy manages to refrain from punching him. Did Mom slip some kind of tranquilizer into his orange juice this morning? "Your mother and I—well, we haven't had a fulfilling marriage for a long time now—not that she isn't a wonderful mother and a great woman..." He pauses. "But, as a man, I have certain needs..."

I want to stick my fingers in my ears and sing loudly, but I'm too shocked to move. How can he possibly think we need to know this? Doesn't he realize the damage he's already done? Poor Troy will probably never be able to enjoy getting a blow job after what he's witnessed! Okay, that's probably not true, given what Kimber has told me about guys enjoying blow jobs, but look what he's done to us! I am now speculating about my brother's future enjoyment of blow jobs! God! Is this what happens to children of sex maniacs?

Thankfully, my brother intervenes. "Just get to the point," he says.

"Sunny and I have grown very close over the years. We have a lot in common and enjoy each other's company very much." My dad pauses. "We've decided to move in together."

"What?" I say. I feel like I'm going to throw up.

"We've rented a townhouse in Surrey. We want you kids to feel welcome there, like it's your second home. Of course"—he coughs into his hand nervously—"it's not a very big place, but there's an extra bedroom. We hope that you'll be able to spend some weekends there with us—alternating with Sienna and Brody."

As predicted, Troy finally loses it. "I'll never go to your fucking townhouse!" He bats my dad's coffee cup off the table, sending it and its contents flying to the floor. "I hate you, you selfish prick!" With that, he runs to his bedroom.

Dad is pale under the fake tan. "He'll come around," he finally says. "I know this is a lot to take in at the moment, but eventually everyone will see that it's for the best."

"Right." My voice drips with sarcasm. "You just keep telling yourself that."

He leans over and retrieves his coffee cup, then heads to the kitchen. When he returns, he has a dishcloth in hand. "We'd better clean up this mess," he says. "Your mother's got enough to deal with at the moment."

Sienna finally calls that night. "Can we meet?" she says, and I can tell she's been crying.

"Of course," I say. "Where?"

"The Starbucks near the movie theater," she sniffs, "in half an hour."

Previously, my mom was reluctant to let me take the car out after dark, but obviously things have changed. I've got a new set of responsibilities now that I'm the only member of the family not locked in my room. "Mom?" I call tentatively through her bedroom door. "Can I take the car? We need to get some milk and cereal."

"Sure," she calls back, without the usual "Drive safely" or "You teenagers may think you're invincible, but I've seen one too many promising lives cut short by driving too fast / talking on a cell phone / fiddling with the radio."

Approximately twenty minutes later I pull my mom's red Mazda Protégé into the parking lot in front of Starbucks. Sienna is already seated inside, pouring low-cal sweetener into her non-fat latte. I order one for myself and join her.

"It's so good to see you," I say, taking a seat across from her and squeezing her hand.

"You too," she mumbles, her eyes welling with tears.

"Are you doing okay?"

"Not really. You?"

"I'm more angry than anything else," I explain. "My dad came over this morning to talk to Troy and me."

"Did he tell you their 'great news'?" Sienna gives a snort.

"Yeah." I imitate my dad: "'One day everyone will see that it's for the best.'"

She rolls her eyes. "Please!"

We are momentarily interrupted. "Tall non-fat latte," the girl behind the counter calls. I hurry to retrieve it and a handful of sugar packets, then rejoin Sienna.

"How's your dad doing?" I ask.

"He's in complete denial," Sienna says. "He keeps saying things like, 'Don't worry, kids, she'll come to her senses.' Like, why doesn't he just accept it and start hating her like Brody and I do?"

"Do you?"

"What? Hate her?"

"Yeah."

"Of course! Don't you hate your dad?"

I think for a second. "Yeah, I guess."

Sienna leans toward me. "Parents are supposed to put their families first. They're not supposed to have affairs and destroy their kids' lives. They're selfish and sick, both of them."

"I know. That's what my mom says."

"She's right. How's she doing?"

"Not good." I take a sip of my latte. "She hasn't worn pants without an elastic waistband since it happened."

"That's so sad."

"What about Brody? How's he handling all this?"

"He's been crying a lot. He's only thirteen."

"Well, at least he hasn't turned into a complete psycho, like Troy."

Sienna stifles a smirk. "What's he been doing?"

"Swearing, punching things... I'm sure this whole mess is going to turn him into a serial killer or something. My dad will be sorry when the TV crews are camped outside his townhouse, asking him if he can think of anything that happened in Troy's childhood that might have sent him on his killing spree."

Sienna can't help but laugh. But after taking a sip of her coffee, she leans in and says, in a serious voice, "Have you talked to anyone else about this?"

"No... Have you?"

"No. When Audrey picked me up at your house, I told her I had a migraine so she wouldn't grill me. And I said our parents had gone out for drinks."

"Good," I murmur. "The last thing we need is the whole school talking about our sex maniac parents."

"Totally. I mean, it'll probably get out eventually, but let's at least wait until after Audrey's party."

I had completely forgotten about the upcoming party of the year, which, given recent events, has sort of fallen off my priority list. "So, you still want to go then?"

"Of course!" Sienna says. "With all the shit that's going on, we have all the more reason to get drunk and forget about everything."

I laugh. "You have a point." I finish off my coffee. "Are you going to school tomorrow?"

"Yeah," Sienna says, "I've already missed a whole week."

"Good," I say. "I've missed you."

Sienna smiles at me. "Me too." She pauses, looking at me intently for a moment. "I want us to make a pact, okay?"

"Okay..."

"We've got to protect our friendship. Whatever our parents do, we can't let it come between us."

Her words send a shiver through me. It simply hadn't occurred to me that our friendship could be in jeopardy. Sienna is my BFF! No, she's more than that. She is my confidante, my link to a social life, the future Dolce to my Gabbana! And Sienna is the only one who can understand what I'm going through right now.

"Definitely," I say, my eyes misting a little. "Besides," I add, to lighten the mood, "this will all be just a bad memory when we're living in our New York loft and partying with Chris Brown or whoever."

"Please!" Sienna says. "Chris Brown will be old news. We'll be partying with the next Chris Brown."

We laugh at this, but then Sienna sighs. "I've got to go. I promised my dad I'd pick up a video for Brody."

"Yeah, I've got to get milk and cereal." Standing, we shrug into our winter coats and then step outside into the night. "So, I'll see you tomorrow," I say.

"Yeah." Sienna rolls her eyes to show that she is not looking forward to her return to Red Cedars. "And remember our pact, okay?"

"I will—BFFs," I say, trying to keep my chin from wobbling with emotion.

"BFFs." Sienna gives me a quick hug and then departs.

With my BFF back at school, things feel surprisingly normal. I once again join Sienna and the others for lunch in the cafeteria. "Where have you been, Louise?" Kimber asks. "We haven't seen you around."

"I've been working on sets for *Rent*," I reply.

"Ahhh..." Jessie says, and then, adopting an announcer-like tone, "The Red Cedars Emmy-winning production of *Rent*!" Everyone bursts into laughter.

Tony-winning, *Tony*-winning, I am tempted to say, but don't bother.

Sienna changes the subject. "So...you guys probably haven't heard about my mom and Louise's dad."

"What?" Audrey asks.

Taking a sip of Diet Coke, Sienna says flippantly, "They've shacked up together."

"NO!" the other girls gasp in unison.

I shoot Sienna a look. What happened to keeping it quiet? What happened to not letting the entire school know that her mom and my dad have found themselves a love shack where they can go at it like a couple of rabbits on E?

She reads my expression. "We'll just tell our really close friends," she explains. "You guys won't say anything, right?"

"Of course not!" Audrey gushes. "Your secret is safe with us."

"Definitely." Kimber echoes, while Jessie mimes locking her lips and throwing away the key.

"So how long has their affair been going on?" Audrey asks, almost gleefully.

"We don't know," Sienna says with an indifferent shrug. "Could be years... Apparently, they have 'very deep feelings for each other' that grew out of their friendship." She sticks her finger in her mouth and pretends to barf.

This is a very different side to the tearful girl I met for coffee last night. But maybe Sienna has the right idea. There's no point letting our parents' sick and twisted choices ruin our own lives. Why punish ourselves by crying and moping about it? "Yeah," I say, rolling my eyes. "They have a lot in common and enjoy each other's company very much."

"On the bright side," Sienna continues, "Louise and I are sort of like sisters now."

"Oh my god!" Kimber says. "That's so cool!" She is looking at me as she says it. Obviously, being Sienna's sister is the cool part and not the other way around.

"Well, you're not *really* sisters," Audrey says, and there is a jealous twinge to her voice.

Sienna looks to me. "So what are we then? Half-sisters?"

"Stepsisters," I correct her. "If they get married."

"Oooh!" Sienna cries excitedly. "We could be brides-maids! We could wear matching pale pink dresses!"

"And tiaras!" I add. To my delight, the other girls are laughing. "We could read a poem," I continue, enjoying my time in the limelight for something other than my drab hair. "Or sing!"

"Something really corny and romantic," Sienna says. "Like... 'I Will Always Love You.'"

"'My Heart Will Go On' by Celine," Audrey contributes.

"Of course, it'll be a little hard to read poetry and sing love songs at their wedding, since we won't be attending." Sienna says, taking a sip of her pop.

"We've disowned them," I add.

"I don't blame you," Audrey says.

"It's totally gross," Sienna replies.

Then Kimber adds, "My dad's new wife is, like, twenty-three and she acts like she's my mom. So...at least it's cool that you're sort of sisters now."

Sienna and I exchange looks. "It is," my best friend says with a smile.

Suddenly, the bell rings. Sienna stands and tosses her pop can into the recycling bin. "Ugh, algebra," she says, making a face. "I've gotta run. Mr. Bartley totally spazzes if you're late."

"I know!" I agree.

"But at least he's got nice arms," Kimber says with a giggle.

"And buns!" Audrey adds.

"Gross! He's a teacher!" Sienna shrieks. Then she turns to me. "Bye, sis!"

"Bye, sis!"

As the week continues, I think I've found the silver lining in my father's desertion of us. Obviously, it's a shame that my mom has been wearing the same pair of sweatpants for ten days and that my brother will likely turn into some kind of sexual deviant because of what he witnessed, but I choose to focus on the positive. Sienna and I are practically sisters! We've been BFFs for years, but now we are more like family. Of course, the parental situation is far from ideal, but I can't help but think that being Sienna Marshall's stepsister might bump me from the periphery of the in-crowd, a little closer to the center.

When I arrive home after school on Thursday, Troy is sitting at the breakfast bar eating a bowl of ice cream. "Where's Mom?" I ask, though I already know the answer.

"She's lying down," he says, shoving a heaping spoonful of Neapolitan into his mouth.

I go to the fridge. "How's she doing?"

He shrugs. "She came out and said hi when I got home, but she says she has a headache."

Obviously, this means I'll be on dinner duty again. I grab a Jell-O pudding cup to sustain me. Then my brother says,

"Oh yeah...some guy called for you."

I nearly drop the cup. I can't believe it's happening already. Sienna and I have only been stepsisters for a few days and already guys are calling me! This is basically the first phone call I've received from the opposite sex. Well, technically that's not true. David Hyslop called once to get my notes from biology class when he'd been out for two weeks with mono. And only last month Aaron Hansen called to see if I had any family members in the medical profession who could get us the numerous syringes we would require as props for *Rent*.

"Who was it?" I ask, trying to contain my excitement. It was probably one of the cute popular boys who has just never noticed me before. I know I'd previously said I didn't like the cute and popular type, but maybe I was too hasty? It's not really fair to judge someone just because they're rich and good-looking. But now, I am on the radar. I can almost hear their conversation:

Cute popular boy #1: That Sienna Marshall is so hot.
Cute popular boy #2: Yeah. Have you noticed her stepsister?
Cute popular boy #1: She has a stepsister?
Cute popular boy #2: Louise Harrison. She's pretty hot too.
Cute popular boy #1: Yeah, she is. I think I'll phone her after school.

But in answer to my question, Troy shrugs. "I can't remember his name."

"WHAT?" I scream. "What do you mean you can't remember his name? Who called, Troy?"

"God! Relax, you fat bitch. I wrote down the number." He points to a pad of paper on the counter near the phone.

"What good is a number without a name?" I grumble, hurrying toward the phone. Grabbing the notepad, I decipher my brother's scratchy handwriting. Below the number it says: Manager, Orange Julius.

My heart plummets. I'd been a fool to think that one of the popular boys had been calling me. I am still lank of hair and big of bone, despite my tenuous family relationship with Sienna. It's time I faced it. There is no bright side to my dad's relationship with Sunny.

Tearing the piece of paper off the pad, I crumple it in my hand. Of all the places I applied, the only one that calls me back is Orange Julius? That's not even going to help me with my career in fashion. And I can't take a job now. Who would make sure we didn't run out of milk and cereal? Who would put the frozen chicken strips in the oven and boil the water for Kraft Dinner? While the average fourteen-year-old should be capable of assuming this responsibility, Troy cannot be trusted around electricity. Blinking back the tears that threaten to spill over, I hurry to my room. I don't want my brother to witness my breakdown.

Later that night, when my mom emerges to nibble on an overcooked chicken finger, she notices the crumpled phone message still on the counter. Smoothing out the slip of paper, she asks, "Did Orange Julius offer you a job?"

"Don't worry," I sulk, staring at my algebra textbook, "I'm not going to take it."

"Why not?"

"Because," I say, "someone's got to make sure we don't run out of food and Troy does his homework and doesn't start torturing cats." She gives me a confused look, so I elaborate.

"The kid's got problems, whether you want to deal with them or not."

While my mom goes to the fridge and pours herself a glass of water, I continue. "Besides, I'm starting to like my hair limp and mousy. It suits my personality."

She closes the fridge and looks at me. I'm preparing for a lecture on my poor attitude, which, I will admit, I sort of deserve, but instead she says, "I haven't been much of a mom for the past couple weeks, have I?"

"Oh, you've been great," I reply with a healthy chunk of sarcasm.

"Things won't always be this bad," she says frankly. "I just need a little more time. I've lost the man I thought I'd spend the rest of my life with and my best friend in one fell swoop. I think I deserve to mope for a few weeks."

I suddenly feel incredibly selfish. "I know," I mumble, on the verge of tears. "You do."

She walks over to face me across the breakfast bar. "I want you to take that job."

"What?"

"It'll look great on your college applications, and it'll give you a little extra money to play with."

"But—"

She cuts me off. "Just because we're going through a rough patch, doesn't mean we should forget about the future. Take the job, Louise."

I shrug. "I don't even know if I want it. I'd rather work in a clothing store or something. And it's not like he *offered* me the job. I probably have to have an interview and everything."

My mom reaches out and takes my hand. "I promise that if you get the job, I'll pull myself together. It'll be the kick in the pants I need to stop feeling sorry for myself and start living again. If you're not here to take care of everything, I'll have to, won't I?"

"I guess. I mean, I may as well call him back."

She gives my hand a squeeze. "You'll knock 'em dead at the interview. I have faith in you."

And so, at 8:00 p.m., I call the number my brother so carelessly scribbled down for me. It turns out to be the cell phone of a man named Grant, who is not the manager of Orange Julius, but the owner of a number of franchises in the area. He asks me to meet him at the Willowbrook location on Saturday morning. While I don't want to be too confident, it does sort of sound like I've already got the job when he asks what size uniform I'll need. Rather sheepishly, I tell him extra large . . . if they have it.

For the rest of the week, I try to remain calm, though I can't deny the life-altering implications of this new job. Obviously, the hair thing is huge, but it could also mark my mother's return to normal life. That means she'll once again prepare meals for us, maybe use the vacuum occasionally, and throw in the odd load of laundry. And, not that she was ever a fashion plate, it will be nice to see her in some presentable clothing again. Once my mom gets herself together, I can go back to being my regular old self. Well, plus grappling with how to have a relationship with my dad now that he's living with my best friend's mom.

I don't have a chance to share the news of my potential employment with Sienna until after school on Thursday.

Sienna, Jessie, Kimber, and I are seated at the Starbucks two blocks from Red Cedars. I rarely join them on these after-school caffeine binges. The last time I did, they all ordered triple venti mochas and tried to outtalk one another for two hours. But since my days of after-school freedom may be numbered, I force myself to go.

We are discussing Sienna's new, and extremely subtle, highlights that her guilt-riddled mother was all too happy to shell out for. Part of me wishes I'd thought of asking my guilt-riddled father to pay for my hair makeover. Judging by his regular Wednesday-night phone calls (I, at least, will carry on a stilted conversation with him; my brother prefers to swear and punch furniture), he'd be all too happy to fork over some money to ease his conscience. But I've gone so far with the job thing that I can't back out now. Besides, I doubt getting my dad to pay would have a positive impact on my mom.

"So," I begin when there is a break in the conversation, "I've got a job interview on Saturday."

"What?" Sienna says, incredulous.

"At Orange Julius," I explain.

"Oooh! Rockin'!" Jessie says sarcastically.

Sienna gives her a look, causing Kimber to say, "I'm, like, totally addicted to the Blueberrathon Smoothie!"

"Yeah," Jessie says with a guilty laugh. "Maybe you can get us a discount?"

"Well...I don't know, but if I get the job, I can ask," I say lamely.

Sienna looks at me. "I can't believe you have to get a job. That sucks."

"Well, I don't *have* to..." I begin, but she cuts me off.

"Your dad is such a prick. First, he deserts you, and now he's making you work for a living. You should be having fun and partying and stuff. And what about your art? You'll never have any time to draw if you're working to support your family!"

I must admit to feeling a little defensive about my dad. Yes, he made an unfortunate choice in accepting Sunny's blow job, but he's not Satan! Besides, I'm working to get highlights, not to put food on the table. But Sienna won't be stopped. "God, just when I thought I couldn't hate them any more, now you have to get a job. We'll never have any time to hang out."

"I haven't even got the job yet! And if I do get it, it'll only be a few hours a week," I say, but obviously I don't want to get into an argument in front of Kimber and Jessie. I calm myself and continue. "My mom says it looks good on college applications. It shows that you're responsible."

"Whatever," Sienna huffs, taking a sip of her café mocha. "It still sucks."

But all thoughts of job interviews, highlights, and my parents' dissolving marriage are temporarily pushed aside in anticipation of Audrey's party. The first step is deciding what to wear. Normally, Sienna and I would be getting ready together, but given that my home is "the scene of the crime," she's not really comfortable coming over. And, as the daughter of his former best friend and his wife's current lover, I also feel a bit awkward facing Keith. So, I am left to try to find an appropriate outfit on my own. Given that I'm planning a future in the fashion industry, I sincerely hope this will get easier. But then, I will always have Sienna's instincts to rely on. When we're living in New York, away from all this parental craziness, I'll never have to get ready for a party alone again.

Once I've selected an appropriate outfit (basically jeans, boots, and a red T-shirt), I need to secure transportation to and from the party. Normally, my dad would have dropped us off and Keith would have picked us up. Obviously, those days are over. Given that my mom seems to favor going to bed at 9:00 p.m. and then getting up again at 3:00 a.m. to watch infomercials, I'm not sure chauffeuring us will fit into her schedule. I decide to take a brave approach.

"Can I use your car tonight?" I ask, only the slightest tremor in my voice.

My mom looks up from an episode of *What Not to Wear.* "What for?"

"Audrey Robertson is having a party." Before she can begin reciting MADD statistics on mixing driving and teen partying, I continue. "Usually Dad would have dropped us off and Keith would have picked us up, but that won't work anymore. I thought of asking you to pick me up, but I know you like to go to bed early these days, and I don't want to have to wake you up to come get me. Plus, I don't feel I can rely on my friends for a ride, because they might be drinking, and I have to be home kind of early because I have my job interview tomorrow morning, so I feel the best solution is for me to take the car."

She looks at me for a moment while processing my rambling statement. Then she says, "Okay. The keys are on the counter. Be home by midnight."

I pick up Sienna in front of her house at 9:30 p.m. and we drive to Audrey's place. When we arrive, we are greeted like visiting rock stars by Audrey and six other girls. At least Sienna is greeted like a rock star; I can't help but feel like a bit of an afterthought. Even Audrey's "Cute outfit, Louise" sounds insincere.

Almost immediately, Jessie summons us to the kitchen with a "come and get it!" Money is handed over and alcohol is distributed. Jessie has an older cousin who seems just a little too happy to bootleg for underage girls. As Sienna receives a six-pack of green apple–flavored vodka coolers, she addresses me.

"I know you're driving, but do you want one?"

Since I'm not much of a drinker, or a driver for that matter, even one would be too many. But in a situation like this, a bottle of booze in hand is sort of like a security blanket. "Sure, I'll take one," I say. "Thanks."

Within the hour, the house begins to fill. I stand near the kitchen and watch everyone file in. There are the usual suspects: Daniel Noran and his group of popular idiot friends who don't know I'm alive; the B-list kids, thrilled to be attending an A-listers party; and, of course, the hard-core partiers who somehow manage to appear at every house party within a sixty-block radius whether they know the host or not. Amid the throng I lose Sienna but stumble upon some friends from my English class. They're not particularly cool or popular, but I feel more comfortable hanging out with them than I do with Audrey's clique. Leah Montgomery and Wayne Jung are also in the stagecraft club. Leah is a really good stage manager and I can see her going places. Somehow, they've managed to wrangle invitations, despite their drama nerd status.

Leah says, "*Rent*'s going to be great, huh?" It's not very cool to be talking about our high-school play while at cool Audrey's cool party, but *Rent is* going to be great, and I kind of want to talk about it.

"Yeah," I say, lowering my voice a little. "You're doing a great job with stage direction."

"And your sets rock," Wayne says.

"Oh..." I shrug modestly, trying to hide my delight, "well, thanks."

Suddenly, our attention is torn from our conversation and all eyes fall on the front door. Despite the raucous music and general cacophony, Dean Campbell and Tracey Morreau still manage to make an entrance. This may be because Dean is by far the oldest person in attendance. With his trucker hat and five o'clock shadow, he definitely stands out. I know Sienna said he was around twenty-four, but I wouldn't be surprised if he was more like thirty-two or something. I wonder if he feels kind of awkward and out of place? I read the front of his green T-shirt: *Suck Mine*. I decide probably not.

We all watch, in a sort of frightened awe, as the couple moves into the room. Tracey exudes a confidence that is almost...menacing. She has hair the color and texture of straw, foundation two shades darker than her natural skin tone, and eyes rimmed with navy liner. A beer bottle is held to her frosty pink lips and there is something really sexy about the way she's drinking it. Handing the bottle to her middle-aged boyfriend, she removes her jean jacket.

I try not to gasp, but it just escapes. Thankfully, I'm standing in a group of stagecraft nerds and various other club joiners who also find Tracey's outfit shocking. "What is she wearing?" Leah Montgomery whispers.

"I—I don't know," I stammer.

Jessie Gray approaches. "It's called underboobage," she explains sagely. "It's the new cleavage."

Well, it certainly is an appropriate name, since the bottom third of Tracey's enormous breasts is hanging out of her tiny blue top. "Interesting," Leah says.

Jessie snipes, "I think it's a bit much. I mean, that look's okay for summer, but it's, like, *March*."

I suddenly remember Sienna's *thing* or moment or whatever she had with Dean Campbell at McDonald's. Hopefully that infatuation was just a brief moment of poor judgment. Scanning the crowd, I spot my friend. Sienna is really taking this "wild girl from a broken home" thing seriously. Judging by the way she's flailing her arms around and squealing with laughter, she must have drunk most of her coolers already. I look at the untouched, tepid drink in my hand. Obviously, I'm going to have to be the responsible one tonight and keep a close eye on my friend.

As Jessie wanders away, Leah clears her throat. "Yeah... *Rent*'s going to be really good." With an impressive show of effort, we stop staring at Tracey's underboobage (except for maybe Wayne) and pick up the conversation where we left off. We discuss the various backdrops, our flamboyant drama teacher, and which of the actors take direction well and which are prima donnas or just too stoned to get what Aaron is saying. I am so engaged that I almost forget to watch out for Sienna. I look around but can't locate her. Excusing myself, I move through the party searching for broken-home girl.

Sienna is nowhere in sight, but I spot Kimber, Jessie, and Audrey. They are standing at the end of a darkened hallway and appear to be deep in conversation. I'm hesitant to interrupt, but then I remember how wasted Sienna is. I've got to find her. "Hey, guys," I say cheerfully.

They all look kind of surprised to see me. "Oh... hey," Audrey says.

"Great party," I continue.

"Thanks."

"You guys having a good time?"

Their eyes dart back and forth to one another. Kimber puts her hand to her lips and bursts into hysterics.

"What?" I ask, instantly paranoid. Why are they laughing? Are they laughing at me? Is this outfit all wrong? Or do I have something on my face? In my teeth? Hanging out of my nose? I run my tongue across my teeth while casually rubbing my nose.

Jessie says, "Should we tell her?"

"It's up to Kimber," Audrey responds.

Kimber calms herself and clears her throat. Her cheeks are rosy from her outburst and her eyes look glassy. She has obviously had a few Mike's Hard Cranberry Lemonades. "Okay," she says gleefully, "tell her."

Audrey looks at me seriously. "This does not leave our group, okay?"

Our group—as in, a group that I am a part of. "Okay."

"Swear," Jessie demands.

"I swear." They are obviously going to tell me something extremely important. While I'm flattered to be included in their circle of trust, I'm also slightly nervous. What if I accidentally spill the beans? What if someone else spills the beans and they think it was me? What if this is all a trick and they are going to tell me I have a booger hanging out of my nose?

"Are you sure you're okay with this?" Audrey asks Kimber.

"Go ahead. Tell her." Kimber looks about to burst with anticipation.

Jessie leans in. "Daniel Noran told Kimber that she could give him a blow job later tonight!"

"Oh..." I scramble for the appropriate response. "That's, uh...well, very kind of him."

Judging by the shocked and appalled looks I receive, that was not it. Damn! I've been invited into their circle of trust and I've blown it. But come on! Is this really great news?

"Uh, Louise..." Audrey says. "He's, like, the hottest guy in our school."

Apparently, this *is* great news. I try to cover. "I know! That's so cool...I mean, great! You're really lucky."

"It's an *honor*," Jessie says.

"It is." Kimber sniffs. "And if you can't see that...well, I just don't know about you, Louise."

Jessie rolls her eyes. "She obviously doesn't get it."

She's right, I don't get it. Daniel Noran is going to *let* Kimber put his dick in her mouth. This is an honor? Cause for celebration? Okay, maybe I'm a little negative about BJs after the whole thing with my dad and Sunny, but come on! I suddenly feel an urgent need to return to the stagecraft nerds, but I can't forget why I came over in the first place. "Uh...have any of you seen Sienna?"

"What are you, her mom?" Audrey remarks. The three of them burst into vicious laughter.

"No, it's just that I drove her here and she seems kind of...well, anyway, have you seen her?"

"Not for a while."

"Okay." I turn to go, then stop. "Well, good luck with... I mean, have fun, you know..."

"Thanks," Kimber says dismissively and then returns to discussing technique or something with her friends.

I edge my way through the party, my concern mounting. Of course I'm not Sienna's mom; but I *am* one of the only responsible, sober influences in her life at the moment. And I did promise her a ride home. Who knows what she could get up to if I don't find her?

Eventually, I end up in Audrey's basement. There are several kids milling around, beers in hand, and a few more playing pool. Down the hall, there are a number of closed bedroom doors. I know better than to knock on any of these. I don't want to interrupt some lucky girl enjoying the privilege of giving Daniel Noran a blow job. But to my right is the bathroom, and I sense that Sienna might be in there barfing up her Smirnoffs. Of course, all sorts of teenaged depravity could be taking place behind that closed door as well, but I decide to risk it. I knock.

"Get lost!" a female voice shrieks from the depths of the bathroom.

"Umm...I'm looking for my friend," I call nervously. There are sounds of a muffled female conversation and then the door swings open. Standing before me is Gillian Weibe in all her intimidating dropout glory.

"Who're you looking for?"

"Uh...sorry to bother you." There's no way Sienna would be in there with Gillian Weibe. Gillian Weibe is like a different species. She dropped out of Red Cedars in tenth grade after she was expelled for spitting on her home ec teacher. "I guess she'd rather go to the school of hard knocks," my mother commented when I shared the news. Gillian is seventeen but looks about thirty (apparently, the school of hard knocks takes quite a toll on your skin). In eighth grade, we were on the same volleyball team, but now...she may as well be from another planet.

"Oh, hi, Louise," she says in a bored voice. She calls to the other occupant behind her. "It's okay. It's just Louise Harrison."

Suddenly, Tracey Morreau's tear-stained face appears over Gillian's shoulder. "Come in," Tracey says, grabbing at my T-shirt with her talonlike fingers. "Shut the door." I allow myself to be dragged inside. I am too afraid to protest.

"Go ahead and pee," Gillian says, "but we're not leaving."

"I don't actually—uh..."

Before I can explain, Tracey dissolves into loud sobs. She hurries to the toilet, where she unrolls a large handful of toilet paper and holds it to her face.

"Are you okay, Tracey?" I ask nervously.

"Obviously she's not okay," Gillian snaps.

Tracey blows her nose loudly. It is strange to see someone with underboobage crying and blowing her nose like that. The look just seems more suited to dancing on top of a bar or riding a mechanical bull. "It's Dean," she says, leaning close to the mirror and rubbing at the streaks of mascara cascading down her face. "I hate him."

I'm not sure how to respond. I want to say something sympathetic but not patronizing. I mostly just want to get out of there without getting beaten up. I finally settle on "Oh, no."

"He's a prick!" Gillian growls.

My eyes dart nervously between the two. Am I supposed to agree that Dean is a prick? But what about when Dean and Tracey get back together, which they are bound to do? Will Tracey be all, like, "You called my boyfriend a prick! I'm going to kill you!" But given her current state of emotional distress, I can hardly disagree. Maybe I could say something ambiguous like, *I'm sure he has been exhibiting pricklike behavior, but—*

My thoughts are interrupted by Tracey. "We had a fight and he just took off in his jeep. And—and...Cameron Littledale saw a g—girl with him!" she wails.

"We'll kill her," Gillian says, punching her fist into her palm, "whoever she is."

A sudden thought strikes terror into my heart. Oh god. Oh please, no! I clear my throat. "That really sucks, Tracey. Uh...I'd better go."

Gillian looks at me, her eyes narrowed. "Who did you say you were looking for?"

My heart is beating like a frightened squirrel as I scramble for an answer that will keep me from being clawed to death by two pairs of hands with metallic purple fingernails. Obviously I can't admit that I'm searching for Sienna. If, god forbid, she was stupid enough to leave the party with

Dean Campbell, then her fate is in her own hands. Yes, we are best friends, but I don't think I should be murdered for her poor judgment. "…Leah Montgomery," I finally say.

Tracey and Gillian look at each other and shrug. "Don't know her," they say in unison.

"She's one of my friends from stagecraft club," I explain. "We're doing *Rent* this year. You guys should come check it out. It's going to be great!"

They look at me like I've just suggested filling their ears with Cheez Whiz. After a beat, Gillian walks to the door and grabs the handle. Before releasing me she says, "If you hear anything about that bitch who took off with Dean, report back to us."

"I sure will!" I say emphatically. Then, in the doorway, I pause briefly. "Well…I hope things get better, Tracey. And…nice to see you, Gillian." With that, I hurry back to the relative safety of the party.

But Sienna is still nowhere to be found, leading me to the obvious conclusion that she has taken off with the middle-aged Dean. What the hell was she thinking? Dean Campbell is old, balding, and dating an extremely tough woman with underboobage. And I have to have the car home in forty-five minutes! What am I going to do?

There's nothing I can do but sidle up to my friends from English class and pretend to be enjoying myself while hoping that Sienna returns before my curfew. But given recent events, it's hard to be optimistic. My mind anticipates the phone call from Keith tomorrow morning. *Hello, Denise,* he'll say when my mom answers. *I guess it wasn't bad enough that Len took my wife away from me; now Louise has taken my daughter. Sienna was found dead this morning, the victim of alcohol poisoning / a car crash / two angry teenaged girls with extremely strong acrylic nails.*

At 11:50 p.m., I can put it off no longer. I'm going to have to go home and hope that Sienna survives the night without me. As I walk to my mom's car at the end of the dimly lit driveway, kids are still arriving, hollering with excitement. Many have cases of beer hoisted on their shoulders. Normally, my early exit would cause me some embarrassment. Only losers with overprotective mommies have midnight curfews anymore. But as I walk to the car, I'm too concerned to feel any shame. Sienna is gone. I've failed her as a friend. And it seems there is nothing I can do about it but confess everything to my mom and then deal with the aftermath.

I'm opening the driver's side door when Sienna appears out of nowhere.

"Hey," she says casually, sidling up to me.

"Oh my god!" I cry, my voice hushed. Anxiously, I glance over my shoulder to ensure that Tracey and Gillian aren't charging toward us. "Sienna, where the hell were you?"

"I went for a drive," she says casually.

"Who with?" I demand, but on second thought, "No, don't tell me here." I glance nervously at the house again. "Get in the car."

Once we're inside, I put the key in the ignition and auto-lock the doors. "You were with Dean Campbell, weren't you? I can't believe you took off with him like that!"

She laughs. "What's the big deal? I'm back now."

"What's the big deal? The big deal is that"—a quick glance toward house, lower voice even further—"Tracey Morreau and Gillian Weibe are going to kill you."

"Whatever." Sienna is actually laughing a little. God, what is wrong with her? She continues, "Do I look stoned?"

Ah, so that explains her laid-back attitude toward her impending torture and death. I peer at her in the darkness. "Not really."

"Do I smell stoned?"

I lean in to take a sniff. She breathes in my face. "You smell like you've chewed about thirty packs of Juicy Fruit."

She laughs again. "One and a half packs actually." Then her voice turns bitter. "It's not like it matters, anyway. My dad's too *consumed with grief* to notice that his daughter is high."

I don't know how to respond, so I focus on backing the car onto the street. When we're cruising through the quiet subdivision, Sienna says, "Can we go through the drive-through or something? I'm starving."

"No, we can't," I snap, sounding uncomfortably momlike, even to myself. "I've got about three minutes to drop you off and get the car home or my mom will freak." Sienna doesn't respond, so we drive in silence for a while. Finally I say, "So, what happened with Dean Campbell?"

"Nothing...We went for a drive...We smoked a joint..."

"Are you, like, going out with him now?"

"Not really," she says breezily.

"Not really? What do you mean, not really?" I demand. "He's got a girlfriend, and have you seen the fingernails on her?"

"They've broken up. She's just having a little trouble accepting it."

"Yeah," I say, "I suppose it's a bit confusing for her since he brought her to the party tonight."

"No, he just gave her a ride," Sienna explains. "It's complicated, but they're definitely not together anymore." She stares out the passenger window. "He's really cool though."

Yuck! Dean Campbell is sooo *not* really cool. I clear my throat. "So...did you guys...you know?" I'm trying not to sound too judgmental about it. It's obvious that Audrey and the girls look at me as a sort of a prude, and I don't want Sienna to think I am. So if Sienna chooses to hand her virginity over to some jerk with a receding hairline and a confused ex-girlfriend, then I will support her decision.

"What?" Sienna is momentarily at a loss and then, "No! No! Nothing like that!"

"No? Not even a..." I try to be cool about this, even blasé, like I know that everyone does it and it's really no big deal, "...blow job?"

"Not even a blow job," Sienna says. We look at each other for a moment and then burst into laughter. While I could easily collapse into hysterics, that isn't a very safe driving practice. I manage to compose myself.

Turning onto Sienna's street, I glance over at her. "Do you really like this guy?"

Without looking at me, Sienna says, "Yeah...I know he's not like the guys I usually go for, but there's just something about him. Like, he's not a boy; he's a *man*."

That's an understatement.

"Like, he's really lived, you know? He hasn't been stuck in stupid Langley his whole life. He used to live just outside of Portland for almost a year. And he has his own roofing business." Sienna finally looks at me. "I don't know. There's just something about him. He's different. And with every-thing that's happened lately...well, I'm different too."

Bringing the car to a stop in front of Sienna's house, I swivel in my seat to face her. I want to say something meaningful, like, "Don't let what our parents did change you. You have to value the wonderful person that you are and know that you can do better than Dean Campbell." But those are my mom's words and they'll just sound corny. Finally, I say, "Well...wish me luck at my job interview tomorrow."

"Right," she says, opening the door. "Good luck."

The next day I'm too plagued by anxiety and self-doubt to give Sienna's downward spiral much thought. As I travel the bricked hallway to the Willowbrook Mall food court, my mom's words echo in my head: *I have faith in you.* Unfortunately, this mantra serves only to heighten my anxiety. What if I let her down? Does that mean she'll wallow in self-pity indefinitely? Will she never have a reason to wear normal pants again? And will I be doomed to a loveless future thanks to my lank, mousy hair?

But it appears my initial instincts were correct when I meet Grant. He's a stout Asian man who, between cell phone calls, hands me a uniform, takes down my pertinent details, and asks me if I can start Thursday at 5:00 p.m. My mom was right to have faith in me. I'm a natural! "Thursday at five sounds great," I say, smiling brightly.

Grant provides me a royal blue golf shirt with a black collar, the Orange Julius logo emblazoned on the breast pocket. I am to wear this with my own black pants. As soon as I get home, I hurry to my room and try the outfit on in front of the mirror. Oh god. Why couldn't The Gap have called me back? The shirt is really big (I guess extra large means man-size) and the color is really unflattering. But I just have to remember that this job is a means to an end. I'm sure the uniform will look much better once my hair is highlighted. I walk to the living room, where my mom is lying on the sofa watching *Trading Spaces*. "Ta-da!" I say.

She looks up. "You got the job!" she says, her voice happy but weary. "That's great, honey."

"Thanks. I start Thursday."

"Wow. That's so soon."

"Yeah." I pause here, considering whether I should say something to prompt her own transformation, like, *Maybe it's time to throw those sweatpants in the laundry?*

But before I can speak, my mom says, "I'm really proud of you, Louise." She gives me a heartwarming smile. "Would you mind making me a cup of peppermint tea?" and turns her attention back to the TV.

The rest of the week drags in anticipation of my first day of work. Sienna is conspicuously absent for three lunch breaks. At least it is conspicuous to me, since I know about her developing friendship with Dean Campbell. Of course, I can't say anything about it for fear that Tracey Morreau might get suspicious and go on a high school killing rampage. Judging by Tracey's much less revealing clothing and her shuffling, melancholy walk, she's clearly still mourning the end of her relationship with Dean. But that doesn't mean she knows about Sienna. Given that my best friend's face is still intact, Tracey's probably in the dark about that.

I spend my lunch hours working on the East Village backdrop for *Rent*. Since my dad's fortieth, Sienna and I haven't spent much time working on our fashion designs, and I don't want to lose my drawing talent due to neglect. While I still pull my sketch pad out on occasion, without my Dolce, I can't seem to draw any clothing. Instead, I find myself sketching nasty caricatures of Sunny Lewis-Marshall.

Unfortunately, my new job is going to cut into the time I have to devote to stagecraft club. I break the news to our drama teacher, Mr. Sumner. "I'm sorry, but I've got an after-school job," I explain. "I won't be able to spend as much time on sets."

Mr. Sumner sighs exasperatedly. (Being a drama teacher, he is very dramatic.) "Well, I'm sorry to say that the timing couldn't be worse. Graham Williams just dropped out as Angel, and Aaron and I are desperately trying to recast. It's not easy finding someone in high school comfortable enough to play a transvestite, you know."

"I'm sure it's not," I say sympathetically.

"And now our best set designer is leaving. We don't need this, Louise, we really don't."

"Well, I'll still be able to help out at lunch."

Mr. Sumner gives an indifferent shrug. "I suppose some help would be better than none."

"It's just that..." I pause for a moment to heighten the impact of my words. "...my father has left us," I say. "I need to get a job to help out with the family finances." I feel even worse after this bald-faced lie, but the words are out before I can stop them. I know for a fact that my dad, while apparently quite comfortable shirking his emotional responsibilities to his family, would never shirk his financial ones.

"Oh, Louise," he says, looking at me with eyes full of pity. He reaches for my hand and gives it an intense squeeze.

"I'm so sorry. Of course we can make do without you. And if you ever, ever need to talk, my door is always open."

"Thanks," I mumble and hurry away. Already I'm wondering how I'm going to avoid Mr. Sumner when I return to school with a full head of highlights and beautifully shaped hair.

But bad news travels fast in theatrical circles, and when I go to my locker after fourth period, Aaron has heard about my resignation. "Sorry to hear you're leaving stagecraft club," he says, leaning against his closed locker.

"Well," I say, feeling guilty again, "I can still help out at lunch."

"And sorry to hear about your dad leaving."

A lump forms in my throat and I focus on my combination lock. Aaron continues, "My parents got divorced when I was seven. It's tough, but it'll get easier."

I can't look at him. If I do, I'm afraid I'll dissolve into tears. Instead, I give a mute shrug. Aaron seems to sense that I'm on the verge of an emotional breakdown. He reaches out and gives my shoulder a little pat. "You're a really great set designer, Louise. But you're right, family's more important." I watch him stroll leisurely off toward his next class. As usual, I can't help but wish that he was taller.

On Thursday, Sienna is once again absent at lunch. My concern for her safety and decision-making abilities mounting, I wait for her return in the school's front lobby. Seconds before the bell rings, my worst suspicions are confirmed when I hear the loud rumble of Dean Campbell's primer-colored jeep. It pulls up out front and Sienna stumbles out of the passenger door.

"What are you doing?" I growl, holding the door open for her.

"What?" she says, through an enormous wad of Juicy Fruit.

"What do you mean—what? Tracey Morreau could have seen you with Dean."

Sienna makes some dismissive spitting noise with her lips.

Though I agree that Tracey Morreau is slightly less frightening now that she is sniveling all the time and mumbling to herself, Sienna's lack of concern for her personal safety can only mean one thing. "You're stoned again, aren't you?"

"No!"

I lean in close and smell her breath. Through the fruity gum, I get a distinctive whiff of beer. "Oh my god! You're drunk!"

As usual, Sienna rolls her eyes at my completely justified concern. "I'm not drunk. I had a couple of drinks."

"At *lunch*?"

She shrugs, attempting to walk past me. "Lots of people drink at lunch."

"Not eleventh-graders!" I say, grabbing her arm. Technically, this is not true. There are many lunchtime drinkers at Red Cedars, but most of them have serious issues, like kleptomania and rage at authority figures.

Sienna slowly extracts her arm. "Will you calm down? Dean and I had lunch and a couple of beers. It's no big deal."

"Suddenly, you're drinking at lunch and it's no big deal?" I snap. "What's going on with you?"

"Nothing, *Mom!*" she says venomously. I recoil from her words as if she'd slapped me. It's one thing when the other girls mock my sensible and responsible (a.k.a. mothering) tendencies, but this is Sienna! She's not supposed to turn on me.

Sienna doesn't apologize. She just says, "We'd better get to class. We're already late."

After school, as I change into my Orange Julius uniform, I vow to put the day's unpleasantness behind me. And maybe Sienna is right. Having a couple of drinks at lunch is not that big a deal. When we live in New York, we'll probably drink at lunch all the time. Sienna is just...practicing, I guess. But my negative thoughts are harder to shake than I anticipated. It doesn't help that I look like a complete dork in this uniform. And what's worse, my mom has obviously welched on our deal. I had assumed that the news of my employment would be met with a symbolic burning of the sweatpants or something. This is supposed to be a new chapter of her life as well. But as I head to the bus stop, she only tears her eyes from *Dr. Phil* long enough to say, "Good luck, honey."

When I arrive at Willowbrook, I take a deep breath and approach the booth. "Hi," I say to the lone occupant, a girl of about eighteen with bright red hair and an unfortunate complexion. "I'm Louise. I'm starting today."

"Hey," she mutters, opening the half-door to let me inside. She hands me a rectangular plastic pin. "Put this on."

It says: *Please be patient. I'm new.*

As I fasten it to my breast pocket, I read her pin: *Hello. My name is Jackie.*

"Russell is supposed to be training you," she says, "but he had to make a phone call or something. He's probably just shopping. He's such a slacker."

"Oh." I laugh nervously.

"So, I guess I can show you some stuff." She looks around, seemingly at a loss as to where to start. "The frozen stuff is there." She indicates the freezer with a wave of her hand. "The powders and stuff are here..." she halfheartedly gestures to a row of plastic bins affixed to the wall. "Cash register...blenders...hot dog machine..."

This is training? God, I hope that Russell guy gets back here soon. Jackie leaves me to attend to a customer and I take a deep, calming breath. Okay, it's apparent that I'm going to have to learn by example. I watch intently as my coworker ladles syrupy strawberries into an ice-filled blender.

Suddenly, there's a presence behind me. Jackie shoots a look over my shoulder. "It's about time," she grumbles.

I turn to face the returning Russell, whom I sincerely hope will be a more hands-on trainer than Jackie. But what meets my eyes steals my breath away. Oh god! I suddenly feel a little faint. My first day of work and now I am faced with this. Russell, my coworker and trainer, is the most gorgeous guy I have ever seen!

"You must be Louise," he says, giving me a slow, crooked, young-Elvis type of grin.

My cheeks are on fire. "Yes. Hi."

"Russell Finney. Nice to meet you." He holds out his hand. Oh god, he wants me to touch his hand! To touch his skin, that warm, caramel-colored skin that is covering his body. That strong, taut body that looks hot even encased in an Orange Julius uniform! God, I've really got to get this shirt taken in. Bravely, I stick out my hand and he takes it. Luckily, I don't suffer a seizure from the jolt of electricity his touch sends through me.

Jackie interrupts the moment. "You'd better get training her. It's going to be super busy in about an hour."

It takes every bit of strength I have to focus on the task at hand. Luckily, Russell is such a good teacher that I'm feeling infinitely more capable as our training session progresses. He is also witty and charming, making the tasks painless and even fun. Of course, being mauled by a grizzly bear would be painless and fun if I could stare at Russell's chiseled cheekbones, his khaki-colored eyes, and soft, light brown hair. There's something so perfect, almost pretty about him, like a young Brad Pitt. I have found him! Here at Orange Julius, I have found "my type"!

Eventually, Russell says, "You're a quick learner, Louise. I think you're ready for your first customer."

"Really? Do you think so?" I gush, my face getting all hot and red again. "Well, you did such a great job training me so...maybe I can try." Judging by the roll of Jackie's eyes, I'm laying it on a bit thick. But it's true. He did do a great job training me, and I feel ready. I serve my first customer a Raspberry Julius and a jumbo dog without mishap. This just might be the greatest after-school job a girl has ever had!

Jackie is off at seven, leaving Russell and me alone. Of course, we're not *alone* alone. There are approximately two hundred people in the food court, but still, I feel there is something intimate about being the only two behind the Orange Julius counter. But I can't let our chemistry distract me. I'm new at this and I can't afford to screw up. There's no need for concern though. Russell and I seamlessly assemble hot dogs and blend smoothies, like a well-oiled machine. What a team!

When the dinner rush has slowed, Russell makes himself a hot dog. "Want one?" he asks.

"Are we allowed?" It might sound lame, but I can't risk being fired for hot dog stealing. This job is more important to me than ever.

Russell says, "We can just say we dropped a couple dogs on the floor."

I can't do it. "I'm not really hungry," I say, then change the subject. "So, how long have you been working here?"

He slathers mustard on his hot dog. "I moved here from Phoenix six months ago. I've been at OJ for about four."

Phoenix. How exotic.

"My dad was a golf pro in Phoenix," Russell says. "One day he was helping this tourist lady perfect her swing and then next thing you know...he's moved to Langley and he's living with her."

"He sounds a lot like my dad," I say. God, we have so much in common.

"Your parents split up?" Russell asks.

"Yeah," I say almost thankfully. I mean, I'm not happy about everything that's happened, but at least it's providing me with a bonding moment with Russell.

"Mine split when I was thirteen," Russell explains, taking a bite of his hot dog. "My dad moved up here, and my younger brother and I stayed with my mom."

"Was it hard when your dad left?"

"It was weird at first, but he was never home anyway. He was always working...or 'screwing his clients,' as my mom says."

"My dad wasn't around much either. He's in real estate."

"The weird thing was that my parents never really fought," Russell elaborates. "I thought everything was fine, and then one day...she just kicked him out."

"That's exactly like my parents," I say. "Except that my brother walked in on my dad getting a blow job from my mom's best friend at his fortieth birthday party."

Russell nearly chokes on his hot dog. "Your poor mom...and your poor brother!"

"I know. He's going to be such a psycho when he grows up."

"When did all this happen?"

"Oh, like, a month ago."

"That's awful!" Russell says, placing his hot dog on the counter. "You must be so hurt...and angry."

To my horror, I feel the emotion start to build in my chest. I can't fall apart in front of Russell. I don't want him to think I'm an emotionally unstable basket case from a dysfunctional family...even if that's what I am. I take a deep breath. "Yeah ... I mean, my dad basically destroyed my family...and my best friend's family. But then he's still my dad, so I still sort of love him, I guess...in a way. It's complicated."

Russell reaches over and gives my shoulder a squeeze. It's just a friendly squeeze of support, but still, it is caring, physical contact. I feel the tears welling in my eyes and I hurriedly search for the wiping-up cloth.

"Hey," Russell says as I scrub frantically at a permanent mustard stain on the counter, "we've got customers."

I turn and see my mom and Troy. "We'd like to place an order, please," my mom says with mock formality.

"Why of course, madam." I play along. Looking down, I'm pleased to see she is wearing jeans. Actual jeans and a clean sweater! This is such a good sign.

Troy says, "I'll have two jumbo hot dogs and a Strawberried Treasure Smoothie. And make it fast."

"Right away, sir." I reply.

Russell approaches behind me. "These demanding people must be your family."

"How'd you guess?" I laugh.

"Let's see . . ." he says, "your older sister and your younger brother?"

My mom laughs, charmed. "Well, thank you very much, but I'm her mom."

"You must have had children very young."

"Oh yes," my mom giggles, "I was just a teenager." When Russell moves to the freezer, she gives me a look that says *What a delightful young man* and I feel my cheeks get red.

As I efficiently complete Mom and Troy's order, I experience a real sense of optimism. My mom is out of the house and wearing proper clothing. My job is going well so far, and I've just met the most attractive, interesting guy I've met in . . . well, ever. Sure, my best friend is dating a creepy, older guy and meeting him for boozy lunches, but there are worse things, right? Maybe things are going to be okay after all? Yes, we've had a difficult month, but it looks like we're on the mend. Maybe my dad was right—everything *will* turn out okay.

13

Of course I'm dying to tell Sienna about Russell! The next day, I find her at her locker before first period. I'd prefer to talk to her before she is surrounded by the rest of her entourage, and before she's had her daily noon-hour drinks. "Oh my god!" I say as I recount my first day of work. "Russell is so good-looking and still so funny and nice and cool!"

"That's great!" Sienna says.

"I mean, I didn't think you could get all those qualities in one guy."

"Like Dean," she says, and I stifle my reaction.

"Right," I say as enthusiastically as possible. "I guess I never thought I'd find my 'type' in Langley. Like, I always thought I'd have to wait until New York, but now, here he is, at Orange Julius."

"That's so cool." Sienna shuts her locker. "We should double date sometime."

I feel instantly nervous at the suggestion. What would Dean Campbell and I have to talk about? We have nothing in common. Well, we have Sienna in common, but I highly doubt we like her for the same reasons. How does one converse with a thirty-ish roofer? How's business? How's the jeep running? I hear they've made some real advancements in hair plugs these days.

"Oh, well, Russell and I are not even dating. I mean, I just met him."

"But you like him, right?"

I feel my cheeks turn pink even as I affect a blasé attitude. "I guess. I mean, he's just so different from everyone else around here. And I feel like I can talk to him about anything. He's only seventeen, but he's so smart and funny and interesting."

Sienna laughs. "I'll take that as a yes, then."

And I do like Russell, more than I've ever liked anyone. My Saturday shift with him just reinforces my feelings.

"My mom thinks I lack direction," he says, leaning back against the counter, "so she sent me up here to live with my dad. He's a total control freak. He said if I didn't get a job or go back to school, he'd kick me out of the house."

I pause my needless counter wiping. "So you don't go to school?" I ask, trying to sound casual.

"I didn't see the point in starting up here," he says indifferently. "I didn't want to go through the hassle of trying to fit into that whole *scene* again. I wasn't learning anything anymore anyway. So I took the GED and now I'm done."

"What's the GED?"

"General Equivalency Diploma," he explains. "It's a test you take to show that you know everything you would've learned in high school."

"It sounds great," I say, rather awestruck. One test that can replace years of high school?

"It is. I don't know why more people don't do it," Russell says.

"I'm definitely going to look into it." Even as the words leave my mouth, I know my mom will never go for it.

"You should. We could hang out together."

I know he's just being flip and charming, but my heart surges with delight. He wants me to drop out of school and hang out with him. What an excellent plan!

Russell continues. "Once I get enough money saved up, I'm so out of here."

My stomach lurches a little at the thought of him leaving. I mean, we just found each other!

"The suburbs are so boring and stifling. They have no heart, no center, no soul," he says passionately.

"Totally," I agree. God! He's like my soul mate! "Where will you go?"

Russell throws the last bite of his hot dog in the trash. "New York, Miami, London... Anywhere with a good club scene. I'm going to be a DJ," he says, his face glowing with excitement. "DJs are the rock stars of our generation. You can make, like, six hundred bucks a night when you get a following."

"Wow!"

"What about you?" he asks. "You're not planning on staying here forever, are you?"

"God no!" Here is my chance to sound worldly and ambitious and the perfect girlfriend for a superstar DJ. "My best friend, Sienna, and I are going to move to New York. We're going to launch our own fashion label. We've been planning it for years."

"Cool..." he says nodding and looking at me like he really means it. "Maybe we'll both end up there at the same time?"

"That would be great!" I cry, maybe a little too over the top. But how can I not be over the top? I've just met the guy of my dreams, and our plans for the future mesh together perfectly! What is there not to be over the top about?

The more shifts I work with Russell, the more I learn about him. And the more I learn about him, the more I feel some divine force placed him here, at the Willowbrook Mall Orange Julius, for me to find. It's like we can talk about anything, like we've known each other forever! I've never had this kind of connection with anyone before...not even Sienna. By the end of our third week of working together, I realize that this is more than *like*; this is love. I am officially, 100 percent, in love. Finally!

Being officially 100 percent in love has improved my mood and outlook immensely. In fact, I'm feeling so positive and benevolent that I'm even willing to meet with my dad. While his previous attempts to arrange another meeting with Troy and me have failed, I feel it's time to let go of some of the anger. Yes, my dad betrayed and humiliated my mother. Yes, he traumatized my brother to such a degree that he has very little hope of ever being a healthy, fully functioning member of society. And yes, he destroyed two families because of his out-of-control hormones and raging midlife crisis. But what does that all matter now that I have found the guy of my dreams? I discuss this with my brother.

"No fucking way!" Troy growls. I'm afraid he's going to lose it again, but he actually seems quite contained today.

"Look," I say, attempting to calm him, "he's a gross sex maniac, but he's still our dad. He's been calling us every week and...well, Mom's doing a lot better now so...I think we should see him."

Troy is silent for a long moment. "I'm not going to his townhouse," he says. "And I'm not going to see *her*."

"Of course not. We'll get him to take us out somewhere nice. I hear that's the beauty of divorced parents—you can guilt them into totally spoiling you."

Troy says, "We could go to Red Robin for burgers."

"Sure. That sounds good."

So when my dad calls on Wednesday, I tell him Troy and I would be willing to have dinner with him on Friday at Red Robin. He agrees instantly, which I appreciate, since he has always been the kind to check his calendar before making commitments.

My mom offers to drop us off at the restaurant. "I'll be fine," she assures us as she backs the Protégé out of the driveway. "This is a small community, and I'm bound to run into him sooner or later. I'm not saying that I won't have bad days, but I'm looking forward now, not backward." She really has been making great strides in her emotional recovery. Ever since that symbolic trip to Orange Julius three weeks ago, my mom has rejoined the land of the living: getting dressed each day, combing her hair, and actually feeding and caring for her offspring. She's also been spending a lot of time with her friend Judith, a divorced yoga teacher who shares my mom's disdain for makeup and body hair removal. Judith has a whole network of friends who are in the same boat as she and my mom.

Our dad is waiting for us just inside the front doors, so I guess he's not quite as open to running into Mom. While it's only been a month since we last saw him, something about him has changed. It's more than just his out-of-season tan. He looks thinner—and not in a I've-been-working-out sort of way but more in a I'm-wracked-with-guilt-for-what-I've-done-to-you-all-and-can't-eat-because-of-it sort of way. But maybe that's just wishful thinking.

"Hi, kids," he says nervously, reaching out to hug us. I pat his back awkwardly, but my brother remains stiff and unresponsive.

When he releases us, he says jovially, "Our table's all ready. Follow me." At our red vinyl booth there are two large, icy glasses of Coke waiting for us. I feel like I'm on a first date with a boy who is really trying to impress me—not that I have any firsthand knowledge of what that is like.

"So," my dad says when we are seated across from him, "how's school?"

I say, "It's fine."

Troy mumbles, "Fine."

"Good...good." He clears his throat. "And your mother? How's she?"

"Mom's great!" I say exuberantly. "She's really doing well. She's been getting out of the house, hanging out with her friends. And she's looking great too!"

"I'm glad," my dad says softly. With his thin, reedy voice and hangdog expression, there's no denying he feels terrible about what he did. So I was right! But while a few weeks ago his obvious sadness and dramatic weight loss may have seemed like poetic justice, now that I'm so in love and fulfilled, I can't help but pity him...just a little.

The teenaged waiter approaches and we order our meals. Troy orders the largest, most expensive burger on the menu. "And bring a dessert menu," he adds.

My dad makes a tremendous effort to engage us in small talk as we wait for our food. I play along, but my brother is uncommunicative. When we're finally eating, he asks about my new job.

"It's good," I say vaguely. "I mean, it sort of cuts into my schoolwork and extracurricular activities, but I've realized that if I want to get a proper hairstyle, I've got to earn some extra money." Unfortunately, my father is unpracticed in the art of guilt-tripping and this flies right over his head.

When the meal is finished and Troy has completed his Mountain High Mudd Pie, my dad drives us home. In front of our house, Troy piles out of the car with a quick "Bye" and sprints to the door. I linger for a moment. "Thanks for dinner," I say.

"It was great to see you," he replies. "I hope we can do it again soon. Maybe next week?"

"Maybe...I've been working quite a lot."

Again, he misses his cue to offer me some hairstyle money. Instead he says, "I—I've really missed you guys." His voice is hoarse with emotion. "It's been hard being away from you all...harder than I thought it was going to be."

A lump forms in my throat. "Yeah, I know," I mumble.

He reaches over and squeezes my hand, a little desperately. "If I could do it all over again...well, I know I've made some big mistakes and—and I'm sorry for hurting you..."

"It's okay," I say, fumbling for the door handle. Tears are welling up in my eyes and I need to get out of the car. I'm still too angry to let my dad know how much he hurt me, how much I wish our family was still together, and how much I really do miss him. Plus, if I start crying, I sense that my dad will burst into tears too, and for some reason, I'm just not comfortable witnessing that. "Let's talk next week," I say, by way of good-bye.

"I love you, Louise!" he calls as I exit the car.

"Love you too." And I hurry toward the house.

14

The following Monday, my mom practically skips into the kitchen. "I have an announcement," she says. "I've got a job!"

My brother and I stare at her in silence from our perches at the breakfast bar. "Doing what?" I finally ask. Unfortunately, it sounds like I'm saying, What on earth are you qualified to do other than vacuum and make grilled cheese sandwiches?

"I have a psychology degree, remember?" she replies defensively. "I'll be working as a counselor for low-income single mothers at the health authority. I've always wanted to do something to really make a difference."

"You have?" Troy asks.

"Yes, I have," she snaps. "Just because I've spent the last sixteen years taking care of this family doesn't mean I don't have my own passions." She grabs her car keys off the counter. "I'm going to the mall to get some new clothes. I start Wednesday."

I decide to consider my mom's new career as a positive step forward. She's healing, moving on, embarking on a new chapter in her life...She wasn't even all that upset when I told her how emotional Dad had been after our Red Robin dinner. Of course, her cheeks turned a bit pink and she looked a little upset, but she didn't burst into tears or anything. On the downside, her counselor job will keep her away from home a lot more. With me working at Orange Julius, Troy will be spending more time alone. I don't like the thought of him sitting in the empty house, probably surfing the Internet to learn how to make bombs or something. But today after school, I'm finally getting my hair highlighted and shaped by Audrey's stylist. I decide to focus on my upcoming beauty and popularity instead of my brother's future career as the Unabomber.

"I'm getting my highlights done after school," I tell Sienna as we make our way to the cafeteria. Thankfully, Dean Campbell has a big roofing contract, which allows me to at least eat with Sienna before I go work on sets.

"Perfect timing!" she cries. "Audrey's having another party! Her parents are going to Palm Springs for the Easter long weekend."

"What day is it?" I ask with feigned interest. I'm hoping for Friday because I'm working that night and will therefore have a valid excuse not to go. I'm not sure I can bear to watch Sienna get drunk and fall all over Dean Campbell. And what about Tracey Morreau? While she appears to have moved on (just the other day I saw her exit some guy's monster truck wearing an incredibly short miniskirt and platform wedges), the sight of Sienna and Dean together may still send her into a jealous rage.

"It's Saturday."

Damn! My mind scrambles for an excuse. I know,

I'll say my mom is on a single-mother suicide prevention training course and I have to stay home with my deeply disturbed brother. "You have to come," Sienna continues. "I'm bringing Dean. You should bring Russell."

"Oh, I don't know," I say, biting my lip to hold back the excited smile curling my lips. The thought of walking into Audrey's party with Russell on my arm is too fantastic! I can almost see the envious looks of all the other girls, hear the excited whispers: *Who's that gorgeous guy with Louise Harrison? Do you see how he's looking at her? He's so in love! And she looks amazing! Look at her highlights!*

Unfortunately, I wouldn't really be on Russell's arm, since we're not even dating, and, therefore, he wouldn't be looking at me with "I'm so in love" eyes, since our relationship is still strictly platonic. And what if I did bring him to Audrey's party and one of the "experienced" girls offered him an expertly administered blow job? I could lose him forever! "My mom's got a job," I say. "She might be working or training that night. And Troy... well, he's in no shape to be left to his own devices these days."

"Your mom's got a job?" Sienna says. "Where?"

"At the health authority downtown. She's a counselor for low-income single mothers."

"Oh... well, good for her. She really seems to be moving on."

"Yeah," I say with a shrug. "She is."

Sienna pulls open the cafeteria door. "I wish my dad would get his shit together like your mom has."

"He's not getting over it?" I ask as we head to our usual table.

"He's pathetic!" she spits. "He still thinks she's going to come back. Every time they go out for dinner, he's all, like, 'Kids, it's just a matter of time before she comes back to us.'"

I stop in the middle of the cafeteria floor. Sienna halts too and looks at me. "What?"

"Every time they go out for dinner?" I ask. "Your parents still see each other?"

"Yeah...don't yours?"

"No!" I cry. "They don't see each other! They haven't even spoken in, like, a month! It's over between them."

Sienna looks at me blankly for a moment before she says, "Well...that's probably why your mom is moving on so well." And she heads to our table.

After school, I hurry to The Scissor Shack. My stylist, Marco, concurs with the hair assessment of my peers. "You definitely need some layers around your face and some brightening in the crown area," he says in some kind of accented English. "You have very pretty eyes. Let's create a frame for them." I excitedly nod my agreement. Marco is obviously very talented and undoubtedly got his training somewhere in Europe where they know a lot about framing beautiful eyes with bangs.

And when he's finally done, my hair looks really good! It's a subtle change. I mean, no one (other than my mom, who said, "Nice haircut, honey") has even commented. But I'm hoping people are thinking, *Gee, Louise looks great. So well-rested—and does she have a tan?* In fact, with my new hair, I almost feel confident enough to invite Russell to Audrey's party. He's much less likely to ditch me for an oral sexpert with my new 'do!

On my Friday-night shift at Orange Julius, I realize I have no reason to fear losing my potential boyfriend to any of my friends. "Look at them," he sniffs toward a table of popular twelfth-grade girls. "They're so pathetic."

"Yeah," I respond, though I'm not really sure what's pathetic about them.

Luckily, Russell elaborates. "Their whole world revolves around being popular—wearing the right clothes, driving the right cars, hanging out with the right friends...Don't they know that there's a direct correlation between how popular you are in high school and how successful you are after?"

"There is?"

"Yeah!" he says, like this research made the front page of all the papers. "Popular in high school equals big loser in real life."

"Well," I say with a smile, "I'll probably be the next Donald Trump then."

"What? You're not popular, Louise?"

I'm not sure if he's saying this in a mocking way, since I would think it's fairly obvious that I'm not. But when I look at him, it seems he wants a sincere answer. I explain. "My best friend is super popular so I kind of hang on the periphery of the in-crowd. She's really great. She always makes sure I'm included in everything. Like tomorrow night," I say, my stomach dancing with nerves, "there's this party at this popular girl's house, and, well, I'm invited..."

"Ugh." Russell makes a face. "Are you going to go?"

"Uh, probably not."

"If you need an excuse, tell them you're hanging out with a friend from work. We could go to a movie or something."

Oh my god! Did he just ask me out? Well, it's not exactly a *date* date, but he wants to hang out with me on a Saturday night, which must mean something. These highlights really work!

Russell nudges me with his elbow. "Check out the blonde girl in the blue jacket." He nods toward the table of popular girls. "She's totally giving me 'the eye.'"

I glance over casually, and sure enough, Kelsey Gibbons is leering at my coworker. A sick feeling of jealousy wells up inside me, but it's instantly quelled when Russell says, "Get real! You are *so* not my type."

I am so in love!

Of course, preparations for my sort-of date begin immediately. When I get home from work, I try on every outfit in my closet. I'm searching for something a little bit sexy but not too slutty, in a color that will emphasize my highlights. (I didn't spend $180 to have them go entirely unnoticed!) Plus, Russell has yet to see that I do have some semblance of a figure underneath my enormous Orange Julius T-shirt. Sienna's fashion expertise would be greatly appreciated, but I don't feel I can call her. Since I've led her to believe that I can't attend Audrey's party because I will be standing guard over Troy, I can't ask her what I should wear to a movie with Russell. Besides, this is not even officially a date. I shouldn't make too big a deal about it.

The next morning, I buy some tooth whitening strips and moustache bleach. A new outfit would be ideal, but given the amount of money I've spent on grooming lately, it is out of the question. I settle on a black boatneck T-shirt and my most flattering jeans. Since the mid-April weather is still quite cold, I throw a belted gray sweater over top. My mom doesn't even comment on my improved looks as she drives me to the multiplex. She's so wrapped up in her new career and training regimen that she's practically forgotten she has kids. At least she says, "You're meeting Russell from work?" Her voice turns playful. "He's sure a cutie."

"I guess," I reply, staring intently out the passenger window to hide my wide smile.

I'm supposed to meet Russell in the lobby of the massive theater. As always, it's a mob scene, a barrage of sights, sounds, and smells assaulting the senses. Scanning the mass of people, I search for my sort-of date. Unfortunately, I'm a few minutes early, since my mom is meeting Judith at a yoga class and needed to drop me off on her way. I don't want to look too eager, so I find an inconspicuous spot next to the *Street Fighter* game and wait.

Just as I'm on the verge of descending into panic that Russell is standing me up, he appears. My breath catches in my chest. He's wearing a brown suede jacket and jeans, and I suddenly realize this is the first time I've seen him out of his Orange Julius uniform. He is almost too gorgeous! And he completely stands out in the milling masses—he's more stylish, hipper, and definitely more urban. I make my way toward him.

"Louise!" he says and gives me a quick hug. "You look nice."

"Thanks. So do you."

"Do you like my jacket?" he asks, holding out a suede arm for me to caress. "I got it at this church thrift store back in Phoenix. It was twelve bucks!"

"No way! It's gorgeous."

"So..." he looks up at the pixelated sign above our heads running the movies and times, "what should we see?"

"Oh, anything's good for me," I reply. "You pick."

And like the perfect, sophisticated dreamboat he is, he selects a Jake Gyllenhaal movie I've actually been dying to see. God, we are so in sync! "I think we'll both enjoy this," he says, handing me a ticket.

"Here," I say, thrusting some money toward him.

"It's on me." He pushes my hand away. "You get the popcorn."

Finally, we're seated in the dimly lit theater with a few minutes to spare before the show starts. I purchased a jumbo popcorn for sharing and a Coke for each of us. Sitting there shoulder to shoulder with Russell definitely feels very date-like. Unfortunately, since I have no dating history, it's a little hard for me to tell for sure. He paid for the movie, which is definitely datelike, but then I paid for the popcorn, which is a little more "just friends hanging out on a Saturday night." Our fingers touch briefly as we both reach into the popcorn bucket and I feel my heart beat faster. With chemistry like that, this has to be a date!

"I had a big fight with Jackie today," Russell says, referring to our redheaded coworker. "She is such a miserable bitch."

"I know," I agree. "What is her problem?"

Russell shrugs. "You'd be miserable too, if you looked like her."

My cheeks turn pink as I blush. Russell thinks I'm prettier than Jackie. Of course, that's not all that hard given Jackie's unfortunate coloring and skin problems, but still! All the efforts I've taken to improve my looks have really paid off.

"Honestly, if you weren't there, I don't think I could stand that job."

I love him! I love him!

The lights go down and Russell and I sink lower into our seats. It may be my imagination, but I think he leans a little closer to me. The pressure of his shoulder against mine makes it hard to concentrate on the film. Jake Gyllenhaal, usually so drool-inducing, doesn't hold a candle to my companion. Seriously, Russell is *that* hot! My mind wanders again to the is-this-a-real-date quandary. The way he's leaning close to me would signify that it is a date (really, he is almost cuddly), but the fact that he hasn't reached for my hand or anything leads me to wonder if he just considers me a friend. Or maybe it's just too soon to be holding hands? God, I need Sienna's feedback on this.

When the film ends Russell turns to me. "What did you think?"

"Uh...good," I say a little hesitantly. I really have no idea what the movie was about.

"Yeah, it was all right. Nice scenery anyway."

"Yeah."

We edge our way out of the packed theater, through the chaotic lobby, and out into the night. Spring is approaching and it's starting to warm up a little, but still I huddle into my sweater. Russell puts his arm around me and rubs his hand vigorously up and down my arm. Hmmm...arm around shoulders = date; too vigorous rubbing = good buddy trying to warm up cold friend.

"Can I give you a ride home?" Russell offers. "I've got my stepmom's car."

"That would be great!" I reply, a little too enthusiastically.

As he leads me through the parking lot, he says, "We could go for coffee or something, but Tanya likes me to have the car home before ten. She's usually pretty cool, but she's a little uptight about her car." When we reach the vehicle I can see why. Russell's stepmom has lent him a vintage Thunderbird convertible.

"Oh my gosh!" I say, admiring the massive metallic blue body. "This is such a nice car!"

"It's a bit cheesy," Russell says, unlocking the door, "but Tanya loves it. It's a 1966, and she's had it fully restored. I just wish it was a bit warmer out, then we could put the top down."

But I don't need the top down. As Russell eases the Thunderbird out of the parking lot and onto the street, I feel like I'm in a dream. Surely, I'm in some parallel universe where I'm a gorgeous, highlighted 1960s movie star, hurtling down the road in an expensive vehicle driven by my incredibly gorgeous boyfriend. I let my body sink into the leather seat, reveling in the moment. I don't need to look at Russell, it's enough just to feel his presence. As I provide directions to my house, even my voice sounds different, more mature, almost...*sultry.*

When we turn onto my street, my heart begins to beat faster. These last few moments have cemented the idea that this is a date in my mind. Everything feels so incredible, so magical, that it simply has to be! I wonder if Russell will kiss me good night. It would be the perfect end to the perfect evening. My hand fumbles for the lip balm in the pocket of my sweater. Do I surreptitiously apply it before the moment arrives, or will that look too premeditated? I don't want Russell to think I *expect* him to kiss me. It's only our first sort-of date and everything. But my lips are so dry! What if he *does* kiss me and it reminds him of kissing some shriveled, dry-lipped old lady? Not that he would know what that is like, probably, but still, it's not the impression I want to give.

But as we near the house, the state of my lips is suddenly the last thing on my mind. I lean forward in my seat, staring out the front windshield. "What the hell...?" I mumble, watching my dad's Infiniti back out of the driveway.

"What is it?" Russell asks.

"Uh..." But I'm not sure what to say. What the heck is my dad doing here on a Saturday night? He doesn't just *drop by* for visits. In fact, he hasn't set foot in the house since the week after he left. What's going on? It has to be something terrible. My mind immediately goes to my brother. Oh god, Troy's done something psycho! As Russell brings the car to a stop in front of my house, I am already opening the door. "Thanks for the movie," I say quickly. "See you at work."

16

Obviously, the timing wasn't right for the second kiss of my life. (Yes, I have been kissed once before. It was a game of truth or dare in seventh grade when Zoe Martens dared me to kiss Noah Spencer in the coat closet for one minute. Noah had an enormous mouthful of braces that caused him to spit when he talked...and kissed, for that matter. Still, I considered it good practice.) Maybe Russell would have tried had I not been so distracted by my dad's presence, but I can't think about that now.

As soon as I let myself into the house, the stillness seems to confirm my worst fears. Hurrying to the living room, I find my mom curled up on the couch.

"Oh, hi, Louise," she says, her voice hoarse from crying. Her eyes are red-rimmed and her nose swollen and shiny.

"What's wrong? What's going on? Why was Dad here?"

"Come and sit down." Her voice is gentle as she pats a spot on the sofa beside her. Unfortunately, her tone only serves to heighten my panic.

"What's happened? Where's Troy? Has he done something?"

"No," my mom says. "He's in his room. He's upset, but he'll be okay."

With my heart in my throat, I sit down beside her. She reaches for my hand and her eyes begin to well with tears. "Your dad...wanted to come back home. It didn't work out between him and Sunny. She's gone back to Keith and the kids."

"Oh..." is all I can manage to say.

"Your dad thought...well, he thought I'd be here waiting for him with open arms."

"And you're not?" I say slowly.

My mom lets go of my hand and reaches for a tissue. "I've always wanted the best for you kids," she says, dabbing at her eyes, "a home with a mom and a dad who love you. But...so much has changed."

I nod my agreement, even as tears of disappointment spill from my eyes. She's right; everything has changed. We could never go back to being the family we were before my dad's birthday. But still, even after everything he's done, I miss him. Even after all the crap he's pulled, I wish she'd let him come home.

"I'm sorry, Louise," Mom says, passing me a Kleenex. "He's hurt me so much. I could never trust him again."

"I know," I say quietly, "me neither."

"If he'd come back a few weeks ago, it might have been different, but now, I just can't go back to that life again... I can't do it." She blows her nose loudly.

We sit in silence for a moment, each of us dabbing at our eyes and blowing our noses. When I finally have myself together, I say, "I'm gonna go do some drawing."

Mom looks at me. "So you're okay?" she asks. "You understand?"

I smile tightly. "Yeah, of course. I totally understand."

And I do understand. But as I sit on my bed that night, halfheartedly sketching some Picasso-esque woman with three breasts and an inordinately large nose, I feel confused and conflicted. It's not like I expected my parents to get back together, but it's just so final. And what about my dad? He's been dumped, deserted, and cast off! The irony is not lost on me, but I can't help but feel a little sorry for him. Despite his horndog tendencies, he's still a good person.

And what's going on with the Marshall family? How is Sienna feeling right now? Is she angry that Keith accepted Sunny back after all the hurt she's caused? Or is she just happy to have her mom home? Finally, my eyelids start to get heavy and I close my sketch pad. There's no point sitting here obsessing. Tomorrow, I'll call Sienna and find out what's going on. Maybe I'll even call my dad...just to see how he's holding up.

The next day, I try Sienna's cell only to find it turned off. Sunny's return has once again rendered me fearful of calling the Marshall house. I wouldn't know what to say to her if I got her on the line. *Hi, Sunny. I'm glad to hear you got tired of banging my dad and have returned to your family.* And what do I say to my dad? *I'm sorry to hear you've been dumped by your "sex toy" and now your wife doesn't want you either.*

On Tuesday morning, after an excruciating Easter looong weekend, I seek Sienna out at her locker before the first bell. It's imperative that I find her before Kimber and Jessie do.

This is private, family business and should be discussed one on one. When I see her hanging up her stylish black blazer, I suddenly feel kind of nervous. But that's ridiculous. This is Sienna, my BFF. My former almost-stepsister! Shaking off my apprehension, I approach.

"Hi," I say, forcing a casual tone.

Sienna looks up and a flash of something anxious darts across her features. "Oh, hey," she says, putting on a bright smile.

"So...how was your weekend?" I am consciously trying not to chew on my lip, a dead giveaway that I'm nervous.

"Good...Yeah, Audrey's party was super fun. Too bad you couldn't come."

"Yeah...too bad."

"Yeah."

"I...uh...hear that your mom's back home."

Sienna clears her throat. "Yeah, she came back on Saturday night." She laughs nervously. "I guess my dad was right all along."

I laugh too. "I guess so..."

"So...what's going on at your house?"

I know exactly what she means by this. "My mom doesn't want him back."

"I don't blame her." There is something nasty in her tone that stirs a sick feeling in my stomach. But at that moment the bell rings.

"Well...I'd better go," I say, somewhat thankfully. "See you at lunch."

Sienna closes her locker. "Actually, I'm meeting Dean for lunch today."

"Okay...well, see you later then."

"Later."

At lunch I work on sets. With less than a month until opening night, time is running out. Besides, I'm not really in the mood to sit in the cafeteria and listen to the gory details of Audrey's party, like who was given the privilege of blowing Daniel Noran this time. Thankfully, painting the backdrop of a New York loft proves a good distraction. Who cares that my dad is all alone and Sunny has gone back to Keith? Soon, Sienna and I will be living in our own New York loft, focusing on our fashion careers. Hopefully, Russell will be there too, and I can go to clubs and listen to him play, or spin, or whatever DJs do, while we fall more madly and passionately in love with each passing moment.

When the lunch hour is up, Leah Montgomery helps me pack up the paints and stow the drop cloths. "Did you go to Audrey's party on Saturday?" I ask her.

"No," she says, making a face of distaste. "I wasn't in the mood. Raj and I just hung out at her place. Did you go?"

"No," I say, trying to sound casual, "I sort of had a date that night."

Leah looks at me. "*Sort of* had?"

"Yeah," I continue, my cool facade slipping as a smile of pure delight takes over my face. "I went to a movie with this guy I work with...this really awesome guy I work with."

"Oh my god!" she cries. "Tell me more!"

But just then Mr. Sumner flicks the stage lights on and off. "People! Lunch hour is over. Get to your classes before I have all your teachers mad at me."

As Leah and I scurry into the hallway, I say, "I'll tell

you about him later. I've got to go to the restroom before Mr. Bartley's class."

She rolls her eyes. "He'd rather have you pee in your pants than disrupt his precious algebra class."

The white, cavernous bathroom is vacant. I briefly take in my appearance in the large mirror above the row of sinks. Marco's hairstyle is proving a little hard to replicate, but it's still an improvement over my previously limp locks. After a halfhearted fluffing, I head into a stall.

I've just finished peeing when I hear them enter. From my position in the stall, it is difficult to identify the female voices chattering excitedly over top of one another. "I think it's totally great!" one voice says. It is slightly distorted, as though the speaker has something in her mouth. Ah! It's Audrey with her omnipresent lollipop.

"It's, like, super good news," Kimber's voice seconds.

"Thanks, guys," another voice responds, which I instantly recognize as Sienna's. "It's for the best. Brody's only thirteen. He still needs his mom. And my dad's so much happier now."

"I'm so happy for you all!" Jessie gushes.

"He always knew she'd come back," Sienna continues. "I guess he could see that she was being manipulated all along. She was just too gullible and too naive to see that bastard for what he really is."

"He's like a predator," Audrey's voice says knowledgeably.

"A con man!" either Kimber or Jessie adds.

I am momentarily confused. Predator? Con man? Surely they can't be talking about—

"We should put up posters with Len Harrison's picture on them: middle-aged women beware!" They all laugh.

I flush the toilet and that silences them. Hurriedly, I zip up my jeans and exit the stall. I'm not sure what I'm going to say, but I know I can't hide in here and pretend I didn't hear their malicious words. As I emerge, their faces register their shock. "L—Louise," Sienna stammers.

My cheeks are burning with anger and humiliation as I silently stalk to the sink to wash my hands. Audrey says, "We didn't know you were in there."

"Obviously," I mutter.

"Jeez!" Audrey snipes, looking to her friends and rolling her eyes. "Don't freak out! We wouldn't have said anything if we'd known you were *hiding* in the toilet."

"Hiding?!" I whirl on her. "I was peeing!"

"God, Louise." Kimber steps into the fray. "Don't be so emo."

My eyes find Sienna's face. She is standing there, her back against the hand dryer, looking guilty. I wipe my hands on my jeans. "Can we talk—in private?"

"We've got to get to class anyway," Jessie says. "Come on, girls." As they file past Sienna, they each give her arm a supportive squeeze. With a quick glance back at me, Audrey whispers, "Good luck, Si-Si."

I don't know where to begin. I am angry, hurt, disappointed...Looking into Sienna's eyes, I expect to see remorse. But instead, I find hostility and a steely resolve reflecting back at me. This is not the Sienna I know. The Sienna I know has always been there for me, the only friend I could really count on. Finally, she breaks the tension.

"Look, I'm sorry you had to hear that," she says. Her voice is not at all apologetic. "I would never have said anything if I'd known you were there."

"You shouldn't have said anything at all!" I cry. "It's none of their business."

"I was just telling them that my mom's come back home. They're my closest friends. They deserve to know the truth."

"The *truth*?"

"Yeah, the truth. My mom explained it all to us."

My eyes narrow. "What exactly did she explain to you?"

"How she was feeling confused and old. She's almost forty-two, and she wasn't feeling desirable anymore. Your dad totally took advantage of her insecurities. He manipulated and coerced her into having an affair with him."

"Really?" I snap. "From what Troy saw, your mom didn't exactly look like she was being coerced."

"Are you defending your dad to me?" Sienna's voice is shrill with anger. "The guy is a pervert! Even your mom won't take him back!"

Her words are so angry, so hateful, that I can't believe my ears. "Have you been drinking?" I ask, almost hopefully. Maybe this is just her noon-hour beers talking.

"No," she snaps. "And I don't need you judging me anymore. I already have a mother for that."

It's only then that I realize tears of anger, frustration, and something a little like fear are streaming down my cheeks. I am furious, disappointed, and betrayed, but I'm also terrified at the thought of losing Sienna's friendship. I open my mouth to say something, but no words will come. In a way, I'm thankful for this. I would undoubtedly have begged her to remember our pact to stay friends no matter what.

Sienna's eyes are cold and stony, and I can sense the finality of our words in them. There is nothing either of us can say that can undo the damage that has already been done. Sienna is still staring at me, her breathing heavy. Suddenly, she takes a step forward and I'm momentarily afraid she's about to slap me or pull my hair. But instead, she spits out the words "Good-bye, Louise." And they hurt more than any physical blow ever could.

I cry more in the next few days than I did when my dad left us. It all just seems so real now. I officially come from a broken home. My dad is alone, cast off, soon to be wandering the streets in his socks, bottle of cheap wine in hand, muttering and swearing about the blow job that ruined everything. My mom is becoming increasingly absorbed in her new career-woman life, basically ignoring my emotional breakdown and my brother's inevitable descent into psychosis. (Who knows what sick plans he's concocting locked away in his room for hours on end?) None of this would be insurmountable if I just had a best friend to help me through it. But no! My BFF hates me now. And to be honest, I think that's what hurts most of all.

Of course I'm still incredibly angry with Sienna. Her blind belief in Sunny's version of events is nauseating. But the end of our friendship means the end of so much more. It's the end of our hopes and dreams for the future. There will be no loft in New York. No Sienna Lou fashion label. We will never party with Chris Brown or Pharrell Williams or whoever happens to be the coolest person to party with at that time. Of course, I don't really care that much about the partying bit, but it's hard to let go of the dream. All I want is to have my best friend back. I want her to come to me and say, *Let's just forget all the craziness that went on the other day. I'm sorry for what I said, but I was upset and hurt. Don't worry, we'll be BFFs forever.*

But I have known Sienna long enough to know that this is highly unlikely. She does not soften and she does not back down. The whole time Sunny and Len were playing house, she refused to forgive her mother. Even Troy relented and had dinner with my dad—and he was an eyewitness! The fact that Sienna is surrounded by three suck-ups who constantly remind her that I'm a complete loser with a sex maniac for a father makes it even less likely that I'll get an apology.

School has become basically unbearable. And yet again, my mom is acting like some kind of crazed advocate for perfect high school attendance. "I'm not feeling well," I say the day after my fight with Sienna.

"You look fine to me. What's wrong?"

"I think I'm getting my period."

"Do you want some Midol?" she asks indifferently, painting her lashes with mascara (yes, whether it's her return to the working world or her new single status, my mother has suddenly shunned her feminist principles in favor of a little mascara and just a touch of blush).

"It won't help."

She sticks the mascara wand back in the tube and looks at me. "What's really going on?"

At this point, I'm almost wishing I'd gone to live with my dad. The mere mention of the word *period* would have seen me on the couch with a comforter and box of Oreos, no questions asked. Unfortunately, my mom is a little more tuned in. "Talk to me, honey."

My chin immediately starts to quiver. "S—Sienna and I had a big fight. She was saying all these horrible things about Dad to her friends, and—and she wouldn't take them back."

"Oh, Louise," my mom says, taking me into her arms. "This is so hard for you. But you've got to understand Sienna's side of things. Her mother is filling her head with stories about being an innocent victim in this whole mess. Sunny's trying to place all the blame on your dad so she doesn't have to take responsibility for hurting her own family. And of course Sienna believes her. No one wants to think of their mother as a cheap slut."

This is very true. "B—but now she hates me," I sniff. "She's my best friend."

"You've got to take the high road," she says, releasing me and handing me a Kleenex. "Don't stoop to her level by insulting her mom. We both know she's nothing but a tramp, but let's keep those words within these walls. When Sienna sees how mature you're being about this, she'll rise to meet you halfway."

"Okay," I mumble, blowing my nose. "But I also have really bad cramps," I try, "seriously."

"You're going to school, Louise," she says, returning to her makeup application. "The Midol's above the sink."

Those first few days were terrible. It wasn't like Sienna and I had any further altercations; it was more like torture by exclusion. I could no longer eat lunch in the cafeteria. Setting foot inside elicited a series of vicious whispers and giggles from the popular table, the meanings of which

I could safely assume. *There's big-boned Louise, the loser daughter of the town pervert.*

Thankfully, I had stagecraft club to fill my lunch hours. But even there, I'd sometimes see kids glancing over at me, their eyes full of pity. *Poor Louise*, they were obviously thinking, *thanks to her sex-maniac dad, she's lost her cool best friend and has no choice but to hang out with us stagecraft nerds.* Okay, they probably weren't thinking of themselves as stagecraft nerds, but still, it was obvious they all knew about my family drama.

My classes weren't too bad. Sienna and I only had biology together, and she moved her seat to the opposite corner and basically ignored me. I could almost deal with the stares and whispers of the other students. The only class that was really unbearable was algebra. Audrey and Kimber sat directly across the aisle from me and made it their mission to ensure I was sufficiently mortified.

"Her dad can't keep it in his pants!" Kimber hissed, prompting Audrey into hysterics. "Maybe he should be, like, castrated or something?"

If not for the iron fist of Mr. Bartley, I'm sure they would have been throwing spitballs at me.

But now I have survived to Friday, and if my mom's assumption is correct, Sienna will forgive me any day now. Tonight is my first shift at Orange Julius since the big fight. (Unfortunately, it's been a slow week and Grant felt the full-time staff could handle their shifts without me.) I can't wait to see Russell—not just because I am in love with him, but because I know he'll be supportive. He already hates popular girls, so I'm sure he'll be sympathetic to what

I'm going through. As I get ready for work, I take extra pains with my hair and makeup.

Despite my current emotional turmoil, my dreams of a future with Russell have not abated. In fact, they have increased, but with a slightly different tack. I have incorporated a revenge fantasy into them, which has proven to be quite fulfilling.

Russell and I will move together to New York, where he'll become a renowned DJ and I an in-demand set designer for Broadway plays. We'll come home every Christmas though to spend the holidays with my mom and Troy. Russell and I will go out to dinner to have some "alone time," and that's when we'll see her.

"Welcome to TGI Friday's. Can I take your—" She will stop as she recognizes me. "Oh . . . Louise."

"Oh, hi, Sienna," I'll say with only a hint of pity in my voice. "I didn't know you still lived in Langley. I've been working as an in-demand set designer in New York for so long that I just assume everyone else has moved on too."

"No, I'm still here. Without your artistic talent, I really couldn't hope for any kind of meaningful career."

"Oh . . . You remember my life partner, Russell?"

"Of course," she'll say, looking at him covetously.

"Russell, you remember my former best friend, Sienna."

"Uh . . . vaguely," Russell will respond as he leans over to nuzzle my neck.

"So, how have you been, Sienna?" I'll ask.

"Well . . ." Sienna will try to maintain her cool here, but a tear will trickle slowly down her cheek. "It's not easy being a single mom to two boys. Dylan has recently been diagnosed with serious

attention deficit / hyperactive disorder, and Kyle needs psychological counseling for his pyromania. Dean won't even help me pay for his son's ongoing Ritalin prescription, and Steve, the traveling vacuum salesman who is Kyle's father, has just declared bankruptcy."

"That must be tough," I'll say, squeezing her hand. "Perhaps my mom could cut you a deal on some low-income single-mother counseling services?"

"That would be great," Sienna will sniff. "I just feel so alone."

"Well, at least you have your good friends Audrey, Kimber, and Jessie to support you."

"Oh, didn't you hear?" Sienna will say. "They all died slow and painful deaths from a rogue strain of the Ebola virus."

I am still smiling when I arrive at the Orange Julius stand. Of course, I must compose myself before I see Russell. I can hardly confess the source of my glee. He's bound to think it's a little psychotic to be dreaming of our future together at this early stage. Maybe after we're married I'll tell him about my crazy fantasies. He'll probably get a kick out of them.

But when I let myself in to the booth, I'm greeted by none other than Jackie. "Hey," she mutters as my heart sinks to the pit of my stomach.

"Oh…hey," I reply nonchalantly. At least I think I sound fairly nonchalant, considering that my internal dialogue is screeching: *What the hell are you doing here, Jackie? Where's Russell? I checked the schedule, and he was supposed to be working Friday! Why isn't he here?*

It's like Jackie can read my mind. "Russell's sick," she says, manhandling a blender container onto its base. "Or so he says."

With an indifferent shrug, I lean over to stuff my coat

into the bin under the cash register. Lingering down there I blink at the tears of disappointment welling in my eyes. I'm being pathetic, I know, but knowing I'd be seeing Russell was the only thing that got me through this hellish week. Taking a deep breath, I pull myself together.

Luckily, Friday nights are busy enough to distract me from my misery. The hours fly by, a blur of juices, smoothies, and hot dogs. Despite our general dislike for each other, Jackie and I work really well together. Inside, I'm terrified that a member of Sienna's posse will show up to mock and humiliate me, but, thankfully, the night progresses without any emotional torture.

At 8:50 p.m., as we're beginning to close, the phone rings. "Got it," I say, simultaneously lifting the receiver and sealing a plastic bin full of juicing carrots. "Willowbrook Orange Julius."

"Louise?"

"Yes?"

"It's Russell."

A bubble of pure joy fills my stomach, my chest, my head. I am suddenly as light as air. But before I can squeal with delight, Russell speaks. "If Jackie's there, pretend it's Grant calling."

With some effort, I wipe the goofy grin from my lips. "Oh, hello, Grant," I say loudly, glancing over my shoulder at my coworker. "What can I do for you?"

"Are you free after work?"

Am I free? Of course I am free! Suddenly, being a friendless loser has a bright side. "Sure. I don't think that will be a problem."

"Good. I'll pick you up at the side entrance behind the Pancake House in half an hour. I've got the Thunderbird."

"Right. Okay. Thanks, Grant."

And with that one phone call, the whole world is filled with butterflies and ponies.

As I let myself out into the dimly lit, vacant alleyway, I feel like the star of a thrilling foreign film. I'm the glamorous, mysterious woman trapped in a loveless marriage to a ruthless older businessman with ties to organized crime. Russell is my true love, the struggling young musician who would risk anything for the woman he simply has to have. Of course, I'd feel a lot more glamorous had I been able to change out of my Orange Julius uniform, but how was I to know that Russell wanted to take me on a date after work?

Moments later the loud rumble of the Thunderbird's engine fills the air and Russell rolls up beside me. He leans over and calls out the passenger window. "Hey, good-looking! How about a ride?"

"Why sure!" I trill, elated that he just called me good-looking. I hop into the car.

"How was work?" he asks, easing the huge car down the alley.

"A thrill a minute," I say. "You really missed out by calling in sick."

"I was afraid of that," he says, gathering speed as we move through the empty parking lot. "I'll never do it again."

We drive to 7-Eleven and Russell buys two enormous Cokes and a bag of Cool Ranch Doritos for us to share. As we leave the store, I'm desperately wishing that we'd run into someone I know—preferably Sienna or Audrey, although Kimber or Jessie would also do nicely. Ideally, the girl would be on her own, just running in to buy toilet paper or tampons while her mom waits in the car. Unfortunately, the store is populated with complete strangers, except for a portly, balding man whom I vaguely recognize as the guy who coached Troy's peewee soccer team.

Back in the Thunderbird, Russell places his iPod in the dock that's been installed in the vintage car. "Listen to this," he says as a wall of sound fills the small space. I try to bob my head along to the driving beat like Russell is doing. He smiles over at me. "Isn't this awesome?"

"Yeah!" I call back, nodding vigorously. Of course, I'm not about to admit this isn't really my style of music. If I'm going to be the girlfriend and eventual wife of a top DJ, I'm going to have to align my musical tastes with his. And I'm sure with a little more exposure to the pounding beat, I'll learn to love it.

But after forty-five minutes of driving around with Russell's dance music blaring in my ears, my head is beginning to ache. Casually, I reach up to ensure my ears aren't bleeding. As the car climbs a steep hill out of the city, Russell pulls off onto a narrow, gravel drive. "Where are we going?" I cry over the intense volume.

He turns the music down. "Somewhere we can talk."

My breath catches in my throat. Surely "talk" is code for something more physical?

As Russell edges the car along the rutted path, he elaborates. "It's a really cool lookout. You can see all the lights of the city below. Sometimes I come up here and just sit by myself and listen to music." He turns to smile at me. "Tanya told me kids have been coming up here to make out since she was a teenager."

"Oh." I giggle nervously. Really, I'm more excited than nervous. There's no doubt in my mind that I want to make out with Russell. I think about it daily, hourly, even minutely! I just wish I hadn't eaten so many Doritos. Of course, Russell has also eaten Doritos and I still want to kiss him, so hopefully he won't be too turned off by my Doritos breath. Taking a large sip of Coke, I swirl it around in my mouth, hoping to dislodge any chip residue in my teeth.

Russell turns off the ignition and we sit silently for a moment. He's right, the view is stunning. It's no wonder kids have been coming here for years to make out. There are a couple of other vehicles in the area, obviously here for the same reason. It feels completely right, completely romantic. In this moment, there's no doubt in my mind why Russell has brought me here. He wants me.

He swivels in his seat to face me. "So...what's going on with your mom and dad and everything?"

Of course, he may just want to talk. "Well...it's been a rough week," I say. Despite being slightly disappointed that he isn't trying to ravage me, I really do want to talk to Russell. And once I start recounting the events of the past few days, I find I can't stop. He's such a good listener that the words just pour out of me. "And now Sienna hates me," I finally finish, biting on my lip to hold my emotions in check.

"What a stupid cow," Russell says. "I can't believe she's falling for her mom's lies. I mean, it's not like she's eight years old. Can't she see that it takes two to tango?"

"I know! And if you met Sunny, you'd see that she's totally slutty."

"And to talk about your dad behind your back is really low. Girls like that make me want to vomit."

"Me too! I mean, I thought Sienna was different, but maybe she's not."

Russell reaches over and squeezes my hand. "You're better than they are, Louise, and don't you forget it. One day, we'll blow this hick town and they'll all be left behind, living their petty little lives, fighting their petty little fights."

"Yeah," I say, my voice hoarse from the poignancy of the moment. It would be even more poignant if he'd punctuate his statement with a kiss, or you know, maybe try to feel me up or something, but still, his words are enough.

And I cling to those words as I face another hellish week at Red Cedars. Whenever Audrey leans over to whisper to Kimber during algebra class, I replay them in my mind. *Screw you!* I think, sending mental daggers across the aisle into their backs. *Enjoy your petty little lives in your petty little town. I'm better than you are.* When I bravely venture into the cafeteria for a Diet Coke and Sienna and her cohorts greet me with shocked and appalled whispers, I just think, *One day I'll leave this town, and when I come back to visit, you will serve me hamburgers.*

Unfortunately, this new attitude does not make me feel any less of a leper. And while I'm extremely comfortable wishing that Kimber, Audrey, and Jessie would be struck down by a stray meteor, I just can't wish that fate upon Sienna. As angry and hurt as I am, I still miss our friendship more than I can say.

Thankfully, I'm able to fill my lunch hours with final preparations for *Rent*. The production is just more than two weeks away, which means each rehearsal is fraught with high drama. Well, the students are handling the pressure okay, but Mr. Sumner consistently loses it and storms out to the parking lot to smoke a cigarette (or quite possibly a joint) in his car. Leah, Aaron, and I have taken to placing bets on how many times he will stalk out of rehearsal. I won three dollars on Tuesday.

On Thursday, there is a light at the end of the tunnel. I have a shift tonight and will get to see Russell! He has promised me on MSN that he won't call in sick again. The desktop computer remained when my dad left, and Russell and I have been IMing almost every day. This has really deepened our intimate connection. At this rate, we'll be kissing and even having sex before you know it! As I get ready for my shift, I put on an extra coat of mascara.

When I arrive at Orange Julius, Russell is alone behind the counter. "Hi!" I say brightly and then try to temper my delight at seeing him. It's normal to be happy, but I don't want to scare him. "How's it going?" I add coolly.

"Finally, you're here!" he cries. "I've been bored out of my mind waiting for you."

I love him! I love him!

Since it's a weeknight, business is a little slower, giving Russell and me ample time to talk. I tell him about my coping strategies for dealing with the "evil triplets" (Audrey, Kimber, and Jessie) and the frenetic preparations for the upcoming production of *Rent*.

"Can I come watch it?" Russell asks, tearing off bits of hot dog bun and eating them. "I'd like to see your sets."

I have the most supportive sort-of boyfriend in the world! "Sure," I reply, trying to sound casual. "Opening night is May eleventh."

"Cool. My aunt took me to see it on Broadway once.

It was great...really touching."

"Well, obviously it's not going to be *that* good," I say with a self-conscious laugh, "but the director is pretty talented."

Russell says, "I'll really just be there to see your sets."

God, he's awesome.

Our conversation is interrupted as a few customers approach but resumes once they've been served. Russell tells me that his mom has been calling him a lot. "She's 'concerned,'" he says, doing air quotes.

"About what?"

"She wants me to go to college," he explains. "She wants me to be an engineer, like my grandfather. My parents have no respect for my career choice. They'll be eating their words when I'm a rich and famous DJ playing in clubs all over the world."

"Totally," I say. "Your mom won't be complaining when you, like, buy her a car for her birthday."

"She's only going to get a Ford or something," Russell sniffs, "unless she gets a whole lot more supportive."

Our laughter is suddenly interrupted by an insistent voice. "Excuse me. Can we get some service here?"

I turn and my stomach drops. My worst fear is realized. Standing at the counter are Audrey, Kimber, and Jessie. Automatically, my eyes search for Sienna. She is seated at a distant table, glaring in our direction. At least she had the decency not to accompany them.

"Oh... *Louise*," Audrey says, her lip curled with distaste. "I forgot you work here."

"Right," I mutter, my cheeks burning. It's exceedingly obvious that they did not forget and that they are only here to torture me. But what can I do? They're customers, and being rude to them could get me fired. The Orange Julius booth suddenly feels like a cage, and I am trapped, a poor, defenseless bear, pacing fruitlessly while nasty school-children throw rocks at me.

"You look really great in that uniform," Jessie says, and the three of them burst into laughter.

When they've composed themselves, Kimber speaks. "Uh, no offense, Louise, but we don't really want you touching our food. You might get some kind of...pervert germs on it."

More vicious laughter, then Audrey speaks. "Could that guy serve us, please?"

Russell steps forward. "Hi, ladies."

"Hi," they chorus, suddenly sweet and flirtatious.

"What can I get you?"

"Well," Audrey says, leaning on the counter so her boobs are pressed together for Russell's viewing pleasure, "we'd like to order four hot dogs and some smoothies, please."

"What kind?"

Jessie leans in. "Do you have any recommendations?"

"They're all good," Russell replies, "but Raspberry Crush is my favorite."

"Yum!" Kimber pipes in. "Four Raspberry Crush Smoothies, please."

"Unfortunately..." Russell says, "I have a policy against serving evil triplets. And since you don't want Louise touching your food—well...I guess you should head over to Taco Bell."

They gape at him. I gape at him. Part of me is thrilled by Russell's incredible display of valor; another part of me is terrified he'll be fired because of it!

Audrey finally responds. "You can't talk to us that way. We're customers."

"Not if I refuse to serve you, you're not."

"We'll call your manager!" Kimber says shrilly.

Russell looks back at me and laughs. "Did you hear that? They want to call Grant." I force myself to laugh weakly. He turns back to my enemies. "Grant is a very close friend of mine, and he loves Louise. Trust me—if it's your word against ours, he'll be on our side."

The three girls are speechless. They exchange looks of mortification before Audrey finally growls, "We wouldn't eat your shitty food if we were starving to death." Turning on their heels, they stalk off to where Sienna's sitting.

20

That settles it! There is only one gift significant enough to repay Russell for his chivalry: my virginity. I had been hoping to give it to him at some point anyway, and his recent actions have just affirmed my decision. Now it is time to take action. Make a plan. No more waiting for the right moment or for him to make the first move. I'm going to *make* it happen, thus showing my sincere thanks and solidifying our boyfriend-girlfriend relationship.

Luckily, my mom has been going out with Judith a lot recently. I casually ask about her plans for the weekend. "Are you going out with Judith on Saturday night?"

She looks at me as she stirs the chickpea curry. "As a matter of fact, we're planning to go to the arena for an ice-skating night for divorced moms. Why?"

"No reason. I'm just really glad you're getting out and having fun."

Now, I must deal with my brother. "What are you up to on Saturday night?" I ask, perching on the arm of the sofa where Troy is sprawled, watching *The Simpsons*.

"Don't know."

"You don't know? It's tomorrow! How can you not know

what you're doing tomorrow? Don't you have any friends? God, you're like an old man or something."

Troy looks at me. "Shut up, you fat bitch!"

"I'm just saying..." But my plan works. During the next commercial Troy goes to the phone and calls his friend Duncan. From my position at the breakfast bar, where I'm doing my homework, I hear them arrange to see a 9:00 p.m. movie.

All that's left to do now is entice Russell to come over. This shouldn't be hard. His frequent IMs indicate that he definitely likes me. Of course, he hasn't showed much *physical* interest in me, but he probably doesn't want to scare me off. Maybe I send off some kind of vibe? A big-boned virgin vibe—as in *Be careful around the big-boned virgin. If you try to kiss her, she may freak out or faint or something.*

I bring it up during a lull in our Saturday-afternoon shift. "What are you doing later tonight?" I ask, scrubbing at a nonexistent stain on the counter.

"Nada," he says, eating a handful of grated cheese. "I'll probably just go home and listen to some music."

My heart is beating loudly in my throat, but I force a casual tone. "You could come listen to music at my place. No one's home and we've got a pretty good stereo."

"Sure. What time?"

Mentally, I run through the evening's itinerary. My mom is going skating at 8:00 p.m., and Troy is being picked up for his movie at 8:30 p.m. If Russell comes over at 8:40 p.m., this should give us ample time to have sex, cuddle for a while, and be dressed, listening to music by the time my mom gets in at 10:00 p.m. "How about eight-forty?"

"Eight-forty?" Russell laughs. "Sorry, I can't make it until eight-forty-two."

I am a bundle of nerves as I wait for his arrival. I have showered, brushed and flossed my teeth, and tidied my room. Hurriedly, I scamper around the living room, fluffing pillows, picking lint off the carpet, and straightening the coasters. It would be grown-up and seductive to offer Russell a drink upon arrival, but my mom doesn't have any liquor in the house, and I have no booze-buying connections. Instead, I put a bowl of Baked Lays on the coffee table.

The doorbell rings while I'm scouring my mom's bedside table for condoms. In a way, it's a relief not to find any, since their presence would mean that my mom was having sex with someone, which is too disgusting to contemplate. But now the onus of protection is entirely on Russell. I'm sure he'll bring some. Teenagers in Phoenix probably walk around with pocketfuls of condoms. I hurry downstairs to let him in.

"Hey," Russell says, giving me a quick hug. I cling on a bit longer, hoping to segue it into a passionate kissing session, but he extricates himself. "I brought some CDs along."

"Great." I lead him to the living room and the stereo. He immediately pops in a CD and cranks up the volume. "Check this out!" he cries over the thudding bass. "It's a mix out of Europe. A friend of mine sent it to me."

"Cool!" I cry, giving him an enthusiastic thumbs-up signal. Russell starts to move to the beat, his body instinctively catching the rhythm. Oh god, we can't dance! I am not a good dancer in any scenario, and I highly doubt my abilities will be improved by my anxiety over the impending loss of my virginity. Besides, this music is so fast and...

kind of weird. I motion to the coffee table. "Do you want some chips?"

We move to the couch and Russell takes a large handful. Casually, I pick up the remote control and lower the volume slightly, allowing for conversation. "So..." I begin nervously, "I really wanted to thank you for...you know, the other day."

"No problem," he replies through a mouthful of Lays. "Any more run-ins with the evil triplets?"

"No!" I gush. "Since you told them off, they've been completely leaving me alone."

"Good."

"I can't tell you how much I appreciate you sticking up for me," I say, leaning a little closer to him. "It was so amazing."

Russell stuffs a few more chips in his mouth. "It was my pleasure."

"They've even stopped whispering whenever I enter the room. You're like my hero!"

"Oh come on!"

"It's true," I coo. "I don't know how I can ever thank you enough."

He chuckles. "Well, your eternal servitude should do it."

And then I know the moment has arrived. I must make my move now or risk chickening out forever. "I can think of one way..." I say suggestively. Slowly, I move toward him, eyes closed, lips parted for true love's first kiss.

"Louise, what are you doing?" I open my eyes to see Russell cowering away from me, his face contorted in a mask of horror.

"I—I wanted to thank you," I stammer, tears of shame instantly springing to my eyes. "I thought we could—I thought—oh god." A wave of humiliation so powerful that I pray for a brain aneurysm engulfs me. How could I have thought Russell would be attracted to me? He is gorgeous. A young Brad Pitt! And I am hideous, a young...Uncle Leon!

"Hey," Russell says, his voice gentle. "I'm sorry. It's not you. It's me."

"It's fine," I say, wiping frantically at my tears. "I uh...I'm just a little stressed out and not thinking clearly and..."

"Louise..." Russell grabs my hand. "You're a really beautiful girl. And if I'd consider being with any girl, it would be you."

I look at him, confused. "Uh...thanks."

"I'm gay," he says.

"Gay?"

"Yeah." He laughs. "I thought it was kind of obvious."

I'm stunned. "Uh...it probably is...if you know any gay people."

"You don't know any gay people?"

"There are no gay people in Langley!"

"Oh, you'd be surprised," Russell says.

"Well, there's Mr. Sumner, my drama teacher, but you're not at all like him."

"No?"

"He's very...flouncey."

Russell laughs again. "We're not all like that."

I'm thinking, *Well, maybe you should be and save us poor straight girls the confusion and embarrassment!* But I don't say this out loud. Instead, I sit in silence for a moment, processing this revelation. My ego is relieved that his rejection wasn't personal. On the other hand, I have just lost the man I love. All my dreams and fantasies for a New York future with Russell will never come true. And obviously, I won't be able to lose my virginity to the most perfect male specimen the world has to offer.

Russell gives my hand a squeeze. "I should have said something. You're upset."

I squeeze his hand back. "It's okay. I just...I feel stupid." And then to my horror, the tears come, and with them, a torrent of words. "It's just that I thought one day, you and I..." A deep sob shudders through my chest. "I just thought...well...I was sort of—I was sort of in love with you."

Russell pulls me into him for a hug, gently stroking my hair. Ironically, this is the most intimate physical contact we've ever had. I let him hold me until the tears finally subside. Then, wiping my nose with the back of my hand, I pull away and face him. "I'll be okay," I say with a brave smile.

"I know you will," he says. "I'm sorry if I hurt you, but really, it's better this way." He explains, "If we were a couple, we'd be bound to break up. Everyone knows teenage romances don't last."

I nod.

"And this way, we can be friends forever."

"Promise?"

"Are you kidding me?" he says, taking my hands in his. "You're my favorite person in the world."

So I am no longer in love, but at least I'm Russell's favorite person in the world. And since I consider Russell the coolest human being on the planet, this knowledge has boosted my self-esteem. That's not to say that the loss of my romantic fantasy doesn't hurt: it does. And that's certainly not to say I'm not embarrassed: I am! But Russell was so understanding about it, like, straight girls fall in love with him all the time, and really, it's his own fault for being so sweet and gorgeous and not effeminate enough for us to figure it out. And for the first time, I actually feel sort of thankful I'm no longer friends with Sienna. If I were, I would obviously tell her about my disastrous seduction attempt. Then eventually she'd let it slip to Audrey or Jessie, and soon it would be all over school. At least this way, my shame is kept private.

So maybe the remains of my high-school life are not going to be such a nightmare after all? Now that I'm no longer hiding a secret obsession with him, Russell and I talk openly about our plans for the future. He still wants to escape to a major center to embark on his DJ career, and I still plan to attend art school. Russell suggested that we could be roommates, which would be both fun and economical. In a way, he has filled the void left behind by Sienna's unceremonious ditching of me. If I forget for a moment the fact that I recently tried to seduce my gay best friend and will likely die a virgin at the ripe old age of eighty-five, I can almost feel optimistic about the future.

As I sit at the breakfast bar optimistically scarfing down a Jell-O pudding cup, my mom walks into the room.

"You got your hair cut!"

Her fingers reach up to play with her stylish new 'do. "Just a trim," she says, but she's smiling widely. "It was time for a change."

"It looks great," I say.

As I go back to my pudding cup, I realize that I'm not the only one feeling good about the future. We're all moving on. It appears that Troy hasn't been stockpiling weapons while holed up in his room and is seeming almost cheerful lately. As long as he doesn't walk in on one of our parents mid–sex act again, he just may become a fully functioning member of society.

Even my dad is doing better. He left his old real-estate agency (obviously, it would have been a little awkward working with Sunny) and moved to a smaller one. He also moved out of their townhouse and now rents a two-bedroom apartment not far from Red Cedars. The idea behind his relocation was that Troy and I might start spending more time with him. He even equipped the second bedroom with a bunk bed. My brother and I have been seeing him more often, but with school, my Orange Julius shifts, and Troy's soccer games, we don't have a lot of free time.

My newfound sense of contentment has even extended to the breakdown of my friendship with Sienna. After nearly a month of avoiding her like the plague, I decide to launch "operation reunification." I will move slowly, beginning by just catching Sienna's eye. Once I accomplish that connection, I'm sure it will break down the wall between us. I can follow this up with a smile, and maybe in a few days, a brief greeting. From there, we'll have a superficial conversation about our last biology test or something until, eventually, we can talk about the craziness that has happened between us.

Finally, in Thursday's biology class, I am able to grab her attention. To do this, I have to position myself right by the door at the end of class and pretend to be fumbling through my notebook for some missing papers. I hadn't wanted to be quite so blatant, but since Sienna seems to have forgotten I'm alive, it seems the only choice. My classmates file past me and I focus on my fake rummaging. But when Sienna approaches, I look up. It's tempting to say something—a simple hi or how've you been?—but I don't think I should skip the first two phases of the operation. Our eyes connect and I give her the faintest, hopeful smile.

Unfortunately, Sienna's response to this is a look of utter shock and repulsion, as if I've suddenly lost my mind, stripped off all my clothes, and am now doing nude cartwheels in front of her. She pushes past me as I shakily return my attention to my notebook.

Walking out into the hall, I can feel my cheeks burning from a mixture of sadness and humiliation. But I can't fall apart. It's bad enough that Sienna rejected my overture of friendship. I can't be seen crying about it! And then it's like

I can feel her looking at me. I turn my head and see Sienna lingering across the hall. She's staring right at me and our eyes meet, for much longer this time. Hers are not friendly, nor apologetic, and they are definitely not inviting. But just before she looks away, I think I see something in their cool darkness. Could it be sadness? Or is that just wishful thinking?

I immerse myself in stagecraft club for the next few days, trying my best to ignore Sienna. But it's practically impossible. Everywhere I go, she seems to be there: chatting with her evil friends in the cafeteria, giggling in the library, or laughing uproariously in the hallway. But there seems to be something phony about her happiness, almost like she's trying too hard. Again, I can't be sure that I'm not just deluding myself that Sienna can't be incredibly happy without me in her life.

On Saturday afternoon, I go to my shift at Orange Julius. "Hi, Maureen," I say to my thirty-four-year-old coworker. Maureen has two kids and usually takes the weekday shifts, but she's trying to earn some extra money to get a new transmission for her car. Maureen is really nice and far preferable to Jackie, but we don't have a lot to chat about. Unfortunately, this forces me to focus on work. I'm just refilling the hot dog machine when he approaches.

"Two Berry Lemon Lively Smoothies," he says.

"Uh...okay." His trucker hat is pulled down low and his face is covered in stubble, but I still recognize him. The same cannot be said for Dean. Technically, we never met, but surely he should recognize his girlfriend's former BFF? Maybe I should say something? But what? *Hi, Dean.*

I'm Louise Harrison. I used to be best friends with Sienna until my brother walked in on her mom giving my dad a fortieth-birthday blow job. It all went downhill from there, really.

I furtively glance around the food court looking for Sienna, and that's when I spot her. Tracey Morreau! She's sitting only a few tables away. Tracey Morreau, in all her teenaged porn-star glory, is sitting right there. But where is Sienna?

It takes me only a couple of seconds to do the math. Tracey's presence is not some weird coincidence—she's here with Dean! Either Dean is cheating on Sienna or he's broken up with her for his old girlfriend. That explains the sadness in her eyes when she looked at me. That explains the too loud laughter and overly cheerful chitchat with her friends. Sienna has been dumped. Hurray! Hurray!

It's wrong to be happy about this turn of events, but maybe now that Sienna knows what it feels like to be dropped like a hot potato, she'll understand how I feel. Maybe she just needed a taste of her own medicine. She'll probably apologize to me on Monday. *"I'm so sorry I ended our friendship,"* she'll say, wiping at a tear. *"Now that Dean has dropped me like a hot potato, I understand how you feel."* God, I am DYING to tell Russell about this.

I phone him as soon as I get home from work. Unfortunately, Russell's take on the situation is slightly different. "Of course this *should* make her think about how she treated you, but it probably won't. All she's thinking about right now is her broken heart." But as I lie in bed that night and the next, I'm still hopeful for a Monday apology. I'll forgive her, of course, but I won't make it too easy.

"I was really hurt by the way you acted," I'll say. "I don't think we can go back to the way we were before. But I'm willing to start over if you are."

On Monday morning, I feel a little nervous and jittery. I'm not going to obsess about the forthcoming apology. I will focus on final preparations for *Rent*. With opening night this Thursday, there's still much work to be done. Maybe I'll suggest that Sienna come watch, since she'll obviously be sitting home alone crying while Dean and Tracey Morreau hang out at a strip club together. It will take her mind off the breakup.

But I barely see Sienna all morning. On the one occasion when we are both in the hallway, she is talking to one of those interchangeable popular guys whom I find so nauseating. She seems completely enraptured in their undoubtedly vapid conversation and doesn't appear to notice me at all. This is a little worrisome, but I still have a strong feeling she'll be begging for my forgiveness before the day is out.

At lunch, I go to stagecraft club. All the sets are painted and looking really fantastic (if I do say so myself). Leah and I go over our props list, organizing them into scene-by-scene boxes, carefully labeled for the stagehands. "So," Leah begins casually, placing a syringe in the scene two box, "you don't really hang out with Sienna Marshall anymore, do you?"

I hesitate before answering. I guess the answer is no, but that may change by the end of the day. "Not really," I finally say.

"Did you hear that she's going out with Daniel Noran?"

"What? So soon?" I ask, shocked. "But Dean Campbell just dumped her for Tracey Morreau."

"Actually, Sienna broke up with him a couple of weeks ago. I always thought they were a weird pair. He's so . . . *old*."

"I know," I agree, dropping a bag of cornstarch into the scene four box.

Leah says, "I guess Daniel Noran is a better match for her—although I think he's a jerk."

"He *is* a jerk!" I say emphatically, remembering the blow-job privilege he bestowed upon Kimber back in February. God, I can't believe Sienna would go out with him after that. How could someone I was BFFs with, someone I had planned a fashion label and a future with, have such bad taste in guys? At least she's no longer dating creepy old Dean, but is Daniel Noran much of an improvement? As I turn my attention back to the props, I realize something: while our friendship only ended a few weeks ago, I don't even know Sienna anymore.

"I'd really like to come see your play," my dad says on the phone on Monday night.

"You don't have to," I reply. "I mean, it's not like I'm in it or anything."

"I know. But you worked really hard...behind the scenes."

"I painted the sets," I explain. "It's no big deal."

"I'd really like to be there, Louise." After a pause he says, "When's your mother going?"

"On Friday. Opening night's Thursday at eight, but she has a yoga class she can't miss."

"I'll be there on Thursday," he says proudly, like his opening-night attendance guarantees him the father of the year award. "Does your brother want to come with me?"

"I'll ask him and get him to call you."

"Okay. Well...we'll see you at the play on Thursday."

"I'll be backstage for most of it," I say, "but I'll come out and see you at the end."

When I hang up, I feel a little uneasy. I appreciate that my dad is trying to be supportive, but the thought of him at Red Cedars puts me on edge. What if he runs into Brody, or Sienna with Daniel Noran? What would they do? Would Brody defend his mother's honor by taking a swing at my dad? Given that he's only slightly larger than Troy, this isn't very frightening, but what about Daniel? He doesn't look very tough either, but his type is bound to carry a concealed weapon. Of course, it's highly unlikely that any of them would attend the play, but still, it weighs on me a little.

But the final days of preparation are so exciting that I can't dwell on it. Mr. Sumner is totally losing it. "People!" he screams, his fingers pressed to his temples. "We have thirty-eight hours till curtain. Is this a time to be horsing around?"

"No, it's not," I say, trying to ease his stress, but half an hour later, I think I see him weeping in a secluded corner backstage.

Luckily I was able to get Maureen to cover my Orange Julius shifts so I can be at every performance. I'm terrified that if I'm not there to supervise, someone might put the dime bag of cornstarch in the scene one box instead of the vodka bottle full of water. My dad and Troy will attend opening night, my mom will be there Friday, and Russell has promised to come to the Saturday matinee.

Finally, the day arrives. While I'm feeling a bit nervous, I know that Leah and I have props well under control. We both stand back and watch the chaos as the actors struggle into their costumes and receive last-minute instructions from the director. Leah whispers, "I'm so glad I'm not Aaron Hansen right now. I couldn't take the pressure."

I look over at Aaron, who, despite carrying the weight of the entire production on his (narrow) shoulders, seems remarkably cool and collected. I whisper back, "I'm so glad I'm not Mr. Sumner. I think his heart's going to explode."

Just before the curtain is raised, I steal a peek out into the audience. The theater is small—less than one hundred seats—so it's easy to spot my dad and Troy in the third row. Scanning the crowd, I'm relieved to find that none of the Marshall clan is in attendance. And of course, the evil triplets aren't there either. Why would they be? They think the whole production is a joke. Besides, they're probably too busy providing oral sex to one another's future boyfriends.

"Louise!" Aaron hisses, pulling me away from the curtain. "We're about to start."

And the first performance is a triumph! Of course, Lucy Menendez sings completely off-key, but she looks so much like Rosario Dawson that I think she can get away with it. Justin Sanderson forgets his lines twice, but only those really familiar with the script would notice. Backstage we rejoice, hugging and high-fiving. Aaron is definitely the man of the hour. I almost feel like I have a little crush on him—until it's my turn to hug him. There's just no way I could be attracted to someone with such a birdlike build.

When the props are finally put away, ready for the next night's performance, I hurry to meet my dad and Troy. I jump off the stage and make my way up the sloping aisle. The theater lights are on and the rows of red upholstered seats are vacant but for a few straggling sets of parents and grandparents. As I head out the theater doors, I scan the school's lobby for my family. The walls of the large, tiled space are lined with trophy cases and vending machines. I spy my dad and brother near the entrance to the gym. Dad is buying Troy a 7-Up from the vending machine.

"Hey!" I say, bounding up to them, full of glee.

"Hi!" My dad gives me a congratulatory hug.

"Well?" I ask excitedly. "What did you think?"

"Fantastic! You kids obviously worked really hard. And the sets, in particular, were amazing."

Troy says, "Lucy Menendez sucked. She can't sing at all. Other than that...it was okay, I guess. The sets weren't bad."

"Oh thanks, Troy," I say sarcastically. "You're so sweet. I feel like I might cry."

Troy gives me a shove and my dad scoops us both into a you-two-knuckleheads kind of headlock. Just then, the doors to the gym open and a stream of people spill into the lobby. Oh right, junior boys' basketball, *Rent*'s competition for the night. I don't pay much attention to the throng of parents until I feel my dad's arm go tense around me. Instinctively I look toward the doorway and see them: Keith and Sunny. Oh no! I completely forgot that Brody plays junior boys' basketball!

For a brief moment, I think everything might be okay. My dad stands stock-still, his arms frozen around Troy and me. Sunny looks over, her face paling immediately, and then purposefully tears her eyes away. But when Keith's gaze falls upon my dad, his face darkens and his features contort with rage. Before I know what's happening, Keith is charging toward us.

"You cheating piece of shit," he growls as he hurtles forward.

"Run, Dad, run!" I yell. But I guess that's not really the way men handle these situations. Instead, my dad puts up his dukes. With their enormous size difference, the scene is almost cartoonish. It would be comical if not for the fact that my dad is about to be murdered right in front of me in my high-school lobby.

"Don't hurt him!" I scream, though I don't really expect Keith to listen.

"Keith, no!" Sunny tries, but Keith has already landed the first punch. To my dad's credit, he just buckles a little and is not knocked completely unconscious. On the other hand, given that this is not the first time Keith has punched him in the face, he probably should have been able to employ some anticipatory defensive moves.

"You should pay for what you did, you sick pervert," Keith yells, his enormous hands around my dad's neck.

"Please, Keith!" Sunny screams. "He's not worth it!"

Everything seems to be happening in slow motion, but still, I make no move to save my dad's life. What can I do? While big for my age, I'm no match for Keith Marshall. But am I just going to stand here and watch my dad be strangled to death before my very eyes? "Let him go!" I say again. Not surprisingly, Keith doesn't stop.

And then my brother makes his semi-heroic move. At some point, Troy must have shaken his unopened can of 7-Up because just as my dad is starting to turn purple, Troy pops the tab and sprays Keith in the face. Keith removes his hands from my father's throat and rubs at his eyes. "Jesus Christ!"

he yells. By this time, someone has alerted Mr. Bartley, my muscular algebra teacher and the volunteer coach of junior boys' basketball. He's able to strong-arm the temporarily blinded Keith out into the street, followed by a crying Sunny and an upset Brody.

Relief flows through me and I wrap my arms around my dad's waist. A few parents approach to see if he's okay. "I'm fine," he says hoarsely, brushing away their good intentions. "Come on, kids. Let's get out of here."

"We can go through the theater door," I say, pulling my dad by the hand. There's no way we can go through the main doors where Keith is probably hovering, just waiting to pounce.

Emerging into the cool night air, my father leads us quickly and silently to his car. Around the front of the school we can hear the continuing commotion. Keith is still cursing and raging, while someone (probably Mr. Bartley) is yelling something about setting an example for your children, while someone else is threatening to call the police. Without a word, we hop into my dad's Infiniti and peel out of the parking lot.

We drive in tense silence for several minutes. Finally, my dad speaks. "Sorry about that. I'm sure it won't happen again."

"I hope not," I say, suddenly hearing Sienna's version of events being related to the evil triplets.

Troy says, "Aren't you even going to thank me for saving your life?"

"Well, son," my dad chuckles, "I don't think you really *saved* my life, but that was some quick thinking there, definitely."

"He would have killed you!" Troy cries.

"I don't think Keith would have *killed* me . . ."

I jump in, "You were turning purple, Dad. Good thing I took you out the theater exit."

"Okay, okay," my dad says, sounding annoyed. He turns onto our street and pulls the vehicle into the driveway. Putting the vehicle into park, he turns to us. "Thank you both for your heroic actions tonight. If not for you, I would surely be dead or in a coma right now."

He's obviously being sarcastic, but Troy says defiantly, "You're welcome," and unbuckles his seatbelt.

"And one more thing," my dad adds hastily. "There's no need to mention this to your mother. It will just upset her."

I nod, though I wonder just how much my mom would care that my dad was nearly asphyxiated tonight. I mean, neither of them has mentioned the d-word, but it's obvious their marriage is over. My mom seems so happy and carefree lately. Maybe she wouldn't be that bothered by her ex-husband's near-death experience?

As Troy and I walk to the front door, our path bathed in light from the Infiniti's headlights, he says, "Well, that was a fun evening."

"Yeah, a real riot," I say. Inserting my key in the lock, there is just one thought that provides me any comfort. There are only five weeks of school left before summer holidays.

Thankfully, the rest of *Rent*'s run goes off without a hitch, and none of my family members or guests are strangled after the performances. I decide to stay away from Sienna and her crew and keep a low profile until school lets out for the summer. Now that I can no longer spend my lunch hours working on sets, I'll need to find something else to occupy my time. Luckily, Leah Montgomery and I have become pretty good friends over the last few weeks, and I'm sure she'll let me hide out—I mean, *hang* out with her and her friends.

But on Monday, Mr. Bartley calls me into his classroom at lunch. Apparently, he feels that since he stopped the attempted murder of my father, our dirty laundry is now his business.

"Have a seat, Louise." He motions to the first empty desk. Morosely, I sit. I am really not in the mood to rehash Thursday's events.

"How are you doing?" he asks, perching on the corner of his large wooden desk.

I shrug. "Fine."

"That must have been pretty traumatic for you on Thursday."

You think? Just because my dad was nearly strangled to death by my former best friend's father in front of me, my brother, and approximately two hundred members of the student and parent population—why would I find that traumatic? "I guess," I mutter.

"I understand that your father was briefly involved with Mrs. Marshall. That must have been pretty hard to take."

"Yeah," I say emphatically. "It was revolting."

"And how has this affected you and Sienna?"

"She hates me now, of course."

"What about Troy and Brody?"

"They were never as close as me and Sienna." To my dismay, tears begin to pool in my eyes. Oh damn! I really don't want to fall apart in front of Mr. Bartley.

He passes me a box of Kleenex. "Maybe I could invite Sienna in here and the three of us could talk?"

"No!" I cry, dabbing frantically at my eyes with a tissue. "I don't want to talk to her. It wouldn't help. I just want to get through the next few weeks and hopefully this will all die down over the summer."

"What if it doesn't?"

"Well, I only have to survive twelfth grade and then I'm moving away with a friend of mine. We're going to New York or somewhere else really cool."

"Sounds great."

"Yeah...And if next year's as horrible as this year, I might drop out and take my GED."

"I hope you don't do that, Louise," he says sincerely. "You get a lot more out of the high-school experience than just the knowledge you take away from here."

Yeah, a lot more anxiety...I blow my nose loudly. "Can I go now?"

"Sure." He stands up. "But I am going to talk to Sienna about the situation. And I'll be calling both your parents in too."

Oh, that's a great idea. Maybe you could lock them all in a room together and let them kill each other? But all I say is, "Okay. See ya."

"If you ever need to talk, my door is always open."

"Thanks."

Now there's nothing left to do but wait for the fallout. I am really tense over the next few days, waiting for all hell to break loose. Surely, once Mr. Bartley talks to Sienna, she'll launch some kind of offensive. She'll probably tell all her friends that my dad provoked her father, taunting him like some annoying little mouse would a gentle elephant. Len Harrison will soon be considered the town pervert *and* a pestering little dweeb. The whispering and taunting will start up again, and I, his only daughter, will be the one who suffers the most.

And I can only imagine how my mom will react once she gets wind of it all. *I'm suing Keith for the attempted murder of your dad,* she'll say. Or more likely, *I'm suing your dad for undue emotional distress on you kids. He had no right to nearly get himself murdered right in front of you, and if he hadn't been banging Sunny in the first place, none of this would have happened.* Oh god. Sunny and Sienna will be called as character witnesses. Or the opposite of character witnesses—character assassins? Whatever you call people who testify about what a dirtbag the defendant is. The entire school will come to watch. Ms. Foringer will probably bring her law class on a field trip. Everyone will hear how awful my dad is, and Troy and I will never get to see him again—not that that thought is bothering me all that much at the moment.

But somehow the week passes without incident...and the next week, and the week after that. Of course, there are a few stares and whispers. Jessie, Kimber, and Audrey roll their eyes knowingly when they see me, as if they fully expected this kind of violent behavior from someone as deranged as my dad. Still, I find the lack of drama confusing. Mr. Bartley doesn't seem the type to lack follow-through, but it's almost like his counseling sessions never happened. Sienna continues to laugh and chatter delightedly with her friends while clutching the arm of her undeniably handsome but still completely vile boyfriend, Daniel. Apparently, she's not bothered by the fact that her father very nearly murdered my dad in the school lobby. I'm seriously reconsidering any previous feelings of forgiveness toward her.

And my mom hasn't mentioned a conversation with Mr. Bartley either. She's still going to work, spending time with Judith and an ever-widening circle of divorcées, and attending yoga classes. She's still upbeat and energetic, almost like she's unaware that her husband was nearly strangled after *Rent*'s opening night. On the other hand, maybe the thought of Keith killing my dad just isn't all that upsetting to her.

The only evidence of Mr. Bartley's meddling is my appointment with the school counselor. The office secretary interrupts my computer class to deliver a slip of paper to me. In Times New Roman font, it reads:

Ms. Penhall would like to see you at:_____.
Handwritten on the line is: *10:30 Tuesday, June 6.*

I complain about this to Russell as we sit in Moxie's, sharing a plate of chicken wings after our Friday-night shift. "I don't want to talk to a counselor. What's the point?"

"I know," he agrees, plunging a wing into the blue cheese dip. "There is no point. It's not like she can fix anything."

"Exactly! And I don't want to talk about it all again." I bite into a wing. "My dad's a sex maniac, okay. It's sickening, but I've accepted it."

"Good for you."

"And why does the school want to get involved in this? Why do they care that Keith Marshall wants to murder my father? It's none of their business who Keith Marshall murders."

"They just don't want to get sued."

"Sued?" I mumble through a mouthful. "For what?"

Russell says. "Like, if you committed suicide or something."

I nearly choke. "I'm not going to commit suicide! God! Do they think I'm going to commit suicide?"

Russell shrugs. "Kids have done it for less. They just want to make sure you're fine."

"I am fine. I just don't want to keep talking about it."

"Don't worry," he says, pointing at me with his chicken wing. "I know how to get counselors off your back."

"You do?"

"Yeah. The counselors were always talking to me at my high school back in Phoenix. Suicide's fairly popular with gay high-school students."

"So what did you say?"

"I talked about the future—how excited I was to move to another city and start my DJ career. Counselors just want to know that you realize high school is just high school, and that no matter how much it sucks, you have your whole life ahead of you."

"Okay...so I'll talk about our plans to move to New York. I'll tell her I'm looking into art schools."

Russell nods his approval and mumbles through a mouthful, "That should do it."

And it works! When I walk into Ms. Penhall's stuffy, windowless office, I am prepared. I don't even crack under her freaky school-psychologist stare, where she pretends to be interested in what you're saying but is really just trying to assess your level of craziness. Maybe I ramble a bit, going on and on about the special bond Russell and I have and how we're so excited to take on the world together. Perhaps I'm laying it on a bit thick when I laugh and say, "One day, my dad's affair with Sunny Lewis-Marshall will be great material for my one-woman play." But Ms. Penhall is all too happy to buy it.

As she prepares to dismiss me from her office, she says, "It's been delightful talking with you, Louise. It's rare to find someone your age dealing with this kind of turmoil at home with such grace and acceptance. In fact, you're probably handling the whole situation with more maturity than your parents."

"Thanks," I say, but I suddenly feel like crying. Obviously, this could undo the last half-hour of upbeat chatter and make her think I'm suicidal, so I make a hasty exit.

And that appears to be the end of it. The last three weeks of school pass without incident. I spend my lunch hours with Leah and her gang and my free time working or with Russell. My mom continues to socialize and exercise, and my dad continues to call every Monday and Wednesday and take us to Red Robin for dinner when we're free. The whole episode with him and Sunny Lewis-Marshall seems like a distant, unpleasant memory. In fact, it's almost like it never happened at all. And it's almost like Sienna and I were never friends.

24

We are eleven days into the summer break when my mom makes the announcement. "Kids, I need to talk to you," she says, coming into the kitchen, where we're seated at the breakfast bar eating cereal. "Maybe you should sit down."

"We are sitting down," my brother and I reply in unison. Troy laughs, but instantly I'm concerned. Whatever she wants to talk to us about has got to be serious.

"Right, okay..." She giggles nervously, then leans her elbows on the counter facing us. "Umm...so, it's been almost five months since your dad and I separated."

Troy and I say nothing.

She continues, "And that may not seem like a long time to you guys, but your dad and I both feel that it's time to legally end our marriage."

My eyes dart to Troy to see if this news will prompt any reaction, but he looks unperturbed. I also feel accepting of this information. It's not like I've been holding out hope that my parents would reunite. Waaay too much has gone down for that to ever happen. "Yeah," I say, "makes sense."

I turn my attention back to my cereal, but my mom isn't finished. "I'm glad you both understand." She pauses and then says, "I don't know if you realize how much I've grown as a person in the past few months. Honestly, kids, I feel like a new woman. When I was with your father, I'd lost my own identity. I was just Len's wife, Troy and Louise's mother. But now, I'm out in the world, working, making my own friends..."

My brother and I continue to stare, mute.

"So...well, anyway, I thought you should know that I have a new friend, who is very important to me."

A new friend? For some reason, this revelation has created a knot of tension in the pit of my stomach.

She elaborates, her eyes glowing and her cheeks flushed. "He's a really wonderful man, and it may seem like we haven't known each other very long, because, well...I guess we haven't, but we both feel that our friendship has become very important to us. We both feel"—she pauses for a second, looking like she might burst into hysterics—"that we'd like to continue this friendship into the future. I'd like you kids to get to know him better."

For some reason, the knot in my stomach turns over. I'm not really sure why. It's not like I expected my mom to stay single for the rest of her life. I guess it's just a little disturbing to hear that your mother is having a *meaningful friendship* with some man. It's nice of her to try to downplay it for us, but I know what this really means. Obviously, she's in love, which means that she's kissing this guy and is probably going to have sex with him—if she hasn't already. I'm supposed to be the one falling in love and kissing and having sex, not her! It's against the order of nature!

Troy speaks, his eyes narrowed. "Get to know him *better*?"

I look at my brother. He is brighter than I thought. I turn to my mom. "We *know* him?" The lump in my stomach has now risen to my throat, and I'm afraid I may barf. If she's seeing one of my friends' dads, so help me, I'll—

"Well, yes..." she says, all pink-cheeked and girly. "From school. It's—it's David Bartley."

"MR. BARTLEY!" I shriek.

"Yes," my mom says, looking a little annoyed by my reaction. "He's a very nice man."

"He's a *teacher*!" I spit out the words like I'm saying he's a child molester.

"What's wrong with that?" she retorts.

I'm silent for a moment, stunned that she doesn't realize how disastrous this is. At least when my dad was sleeping with Sunny, it affected only Sienna and Brody. But dating Mr. Bartley will affect everyone! It's sort of like she's dating the whole school's dad! I stand up. "I can't believe you'd embarrass me like this!"

"Embarrass you?" she says. "How am I embarrassing you? I've developed a close friendship with a very nice man who makes me feel special and wonderful and who happens to care a lot about you. That's how I met him, by the way. He called me in to meet with him after that fiasco with your dad and Keith at the play. He was concerned about you."

I don't like the way she's turning the tables and trying to make me out to be the bad guy here. She obviously doesn't know—or care—that I was taunted mercilessly about my dad's sex life for months. Now she's gone and developed a "close friendship" with my math teacher!

"Oh, no, that's great news. Fantastic! Congratulations!" I hop off the stool. "I've got to go to work."

As I head to Orange Julius, I'm thankful to have the distraction of work. Russell and I were able to coordinate most of our shifts this week, and I know he'll take my mind off my mom's love affair with my algebra teacher. I am not going to obsess over the field day the evil triplets will have when they get wind of this. In fact, I won't even mention it to Russell. It's an embarrassing subject on so many levels.

We're setting up for the 10:00 a.m. opening when Russell says, "I've got something to tell you." I look over at him placing raw wieners on the revolving roaster and notice a devilish twinkle in his eye. Oh good. He's got something juicy to tell me that will surely beat my mom's news about her future with the wonderful Mr. Bartley.

"What?" I ask eagerly.

Russell glances around him at the near-empty food court. "I've met someone," he whispers.

"Met someone?" Normally, this statement would mean a romance, but given that Russell and Mr. Sumner are the only two gay people in Langley, it seems unlikely. Oh god! If Russell is dating a teacher too, I'll kill myself.

"Yeah," he explains excitedly. "I never expected to meet someone here, but I just looked up and there he was."

"Great," I reply wanly, extracting the berry bins from the fridge. This is just fantastic. Even gay teenagers and single mothers have better love lives than I do.

"He's really gorgeous and totally fit! And he's got this kind of preppy sexiness. I mean, we have more of a physical attraction right now, but I'd like to get to know him better. I think there's a really interesting, unique person deep down inside him that he's trying to hide."

"Mmm..." I busy myself with the till.

"And we already have one really important thing in common—he likes the same music that I do!"

My heart sinks. I lost Sienna and now I'm going to lose Russell. I'm being replaced, I can feel it. And who can blame him? This new guy likes the same music and has the appropriate "equipment." Obviously, Russell will choose him over me. "That's great. I'm sure you two will have a wonderful future together in New York or wherever," I say, sounding like a petulant child.

Russell lets out a laugh. "Louise, are you jealous?"

"I'm not," I snap, trying to quell the tears springing to my eyes. "It's great that you've found someone. My mom's found someone too: my algebra teacher."

"Oh..." Russell makes a distasteful face.

"I know," I say, swiping hurriedly at my eyes while trying to jam the cash tray into the register.

Russell moves toward me. "Hey..." He gently eases the metal tray into its drawer. "This doesn't change our plans. This is just a bit of fun...It's just something to make my time in Langley less painful."

I look up at him, my eyes red and shining. "What if you fall in love? You won't want me around anymore." I realize I'm being melodramatic, but I just can't take losing another best friend so soon after Sienna.

"Don't be ridiculous. This guy's not even out yet. He's hardly going to move away with me."

"Really?"

"Yeah, he says he's 'confused about his sexuality,' which is really just another term for denial."

Relief floods through me. "So who is this guy?"

Russell turns his attentions to the hot-dog machine. "I doubt you know him."

"Try me."

Russell faces me, his expression earnest. "He wants to keep our relationship quiet for now, and I'm going to respect that. If it goes any further, and he's comfortable with it, you'll be the first person I tell."

"Okay," I say. I have to admire Russell's attitude. And now that I know this guy is not a major threat to our relationship, I'm really in no hurry to meet him.

"So," Russell says, with a finality that indicates the subject is closed, "your mom and your algebra teacher, huh? Is he hot at least?"

The first time Mr. Bartley—or *Dave,* as we are instructed to call him—comes over for dinner, it's a little weird. Okay, it's a lot weird. First of all, teachers are not supposed to be invited into your home. And secondly, my mom is acting like a total spaz.

"Okay," she says, fluttering around the table like a butterfly on speed, "Louise can sit here...Dave, you can sit next to me over here. And, Troy, you can sit at the head of the table, since you're the man of the house."

I roll my eyes at her obvious attempt to make my brother feel important. Mr. Bartley catches my look and gives me an understanding smirk.

When we're seated, my mom hurries to the kitchen to retrieve the casserole from the oven. She returns wearing green oven mitts and carrying a large glass dish. "Baked red lentil and wild rice casserole. It might not sound very good, but it's actually quite tasty. And it's so good for you."

"I'm sure it's great," Mr. Bartley says. Then he turns to Troy and me. "Have you ever noticed that your mom's a little obsessed with fiber?"

"No, I never noticed," Troy says sarcastically.

"Me either," I join in.

"Don't gang up on me!" my mom cries, looking positively thrilled.

As we eat the casserole (it really isn't that bad), I can't help but enjoy the evening. If it weren't for the fact that he's my teacher, Mr. Bartley—I mean, Dave—is not a bad guy. He's actually kind of funny. And I have to admit that my mom practically glows every time she looks at him. It's still kind of weird that my mother is dating a teacher, but at least they're not physically affectionate with each other. That would be too much to take.

Two weeks later, Troy and I have dinner plans with our dad. Before we leave, I visit my brother in his room. "I don't think we should tell Dad about Mom and Mr. Bartley. Dad's had a rough year, and it might be too much for him to take."

"Yeah," Troy says, fiddling with a Rubik's cube he will never solve, "I was thinking the same thing."

"Good," I say, happy that my brother seems to have developed some normal feelings recently. "We won't mention it then."

When we're at Red Robin, we keep conversation light, avoiding depressing topics like Mom and Dad's impending divorce, her blossoming new relationship, and the fact that Dad was nearly murdered by his former best friend.

"I'd like to take you kids away for a few days," he says, dipping a steak-cut fry in ketchup. "Maybe camping or something."

"Sure!" Troy, who loves camping, says.

I, who do not love camping, say, "I don't know if I can get time off work."

"I'm sure they can spare you for a day or two," my dad chides.

"Or just you two could go?" I suggest.

"We'll work something out," he says, taking a sip of Diet Coke. "I'll talk to your mom about it when I drop you off."

"You don't need to do that," I say, eyes darting nervously to meet my brother's. With her kids out of the house, my mom and Dave would undoubtedly be sharing a romantic dinner *a deux* at this very moment.

"Yeah, she won't care," Troy concurs.

My dad gives us a look. "I'd like to run it by her anyway. I don't want to step on her toes—you know, in case she has plans with you kids."

"She doesn't," I say quickly. "We never have any plans with her."

"That's true," Troy adds hurriedly. "She works all the time now. We never do anything together."

My dad laughs and shakes his head, turning his attention back to his burger.

On the drive home, my heart is in my throat. I don't know if I can take another family confrontation. At least when my dad was up against Keith Marshall, he'd had the advantage of speed, but Mr. Bartley is much spryer, and he's muscular. Len won't have a chance! And who will break it up before Dave kills him? Troy? As if! I just hope my dad will remember Dave's lifesaving role in his last skirmish and think twice about challenging him.

When we pull into the driveway, my dad puts the Infiniti into park and turns off the ignition. "Looks like mom's asleep," Troy says, indicating the single light shining from the kitchen. "We'd better not disturb her."

My dad looks at me in the passenger seat and then over his shoulder to Troy in the back. "I know about your mom and Dave Bartley."

"You do?" we say in unison.

"It's a small town. She knew I'd find out eventually, so she called me and told me."

"A—And you're okay with it?" I stammer.

For the first time, there is a glint of sadness in his eyes. "I have to accept the fact that your mother is ready to end our marriage and move on. She's a wonderful woman and she deserves to be happy."

"Umm...okay."

"So," he says, rubbing his palms together, "let's talk to her about that camping trip."

With my father's acceptance, my mom's new relationship suddenly doesn't seem so devastating. Dave is a nice guy and he obviously makes her happy. So maybe it's not so bad?

❦

And if I'm okay with my mom's new relationship, then I should be able to accept Russell's new sort-of boyfriend too. When we're sitting in his basement listening to music one Friday night, I summon the courage to ask him about it. "How are things with that guy you're seeing?" I ask casually.

Russell plays with the laptop in his lap, moving from one bass-pounding techno song to another indistinguishable one. "I'm not seeing him anymore."

"Oh?" Oops. I hope I don't sound too happy.

"He's trying to convince himself that he's straight."

"And you don't think he is?"

Russell looks at me frankly. "Trust me. He's not."

"Well... that's too bad."

"It's too bad for him," Russell says flippantly, inspecting the playlist on the screen. "He's going to live a lie until he can't take it any longer and then he's going to break some poor girl's heart."

We are silent for a while, immersing ourselves in the music. At least Russell is immersing himself in the music; I'm still thinking of the appropriate response. I'm afraid to speak in case my incredible happiness at having Russell all to myself again comes out. Not that his previous relationship substantially cut into our time together, but it's more of a symbolic thing. With Russell unattached, it's sort of like I have a boyfriend—without the sex, of course.

Finally I say, "He'll be just like that gay senator in New Jersey or wherever, who had a wife and two kids when he finally came out."

Russell looks at me pointedly. "He was the governor. And I don't know if my guy is really the political type."

Internally, I flinch at the "my guy" reference, but outwardly I smile sadly. "It's a shame," I say.

"Yeah," Russell mumbles, and I can tell he's trying hard to mask his sadness. Then, turning up the volume, he says, "Check out the sampling on this track."

And so my summer progresses... I work, I spend time with Russell, and occasionally I meet Leah Montgomery and some of the gang for pizza or coffee. Only once do I see Sienna, and it's from a distance. Troy and I are renting a video when she and Daniel Noran walk into Blockbuster. I'm already at the till and just about to exit when they arrive. Sienna is looking in the other direction, but Daniel Noran looks right at me. Luckily, he's such a self-absorbed dink that he has no idea who I am. But I'm surprised and a little disturbed by the intensity of my reaction to this Sienna sighting. I have Russell now. I don't need her anymore. So why did I experience such a pang in my heart when she walked in?

As my brother and I drive home from the video store, I decide to focus on the positive. After the tumultuous months my family has endured, we've finally hit some smooth sailing. My mom is happy, my dad is accepting, and my brother hasn't punched a wall since March. I slowly maneuver the car into the driveway. Before I turn off the ignition, I turn to face Troy. "We've had a rough year, but things are finally looking up, aren't they?" I smile at him.

My brother gapes at me like I've just proposed marriage to him and hops out of the car without a word. But this doesn't dampen my hopeful mood. Despite my lingering sadness about Sienna, I am definitely moving on with my life.

Three weeks before school resumes, my mom summons Troy and me to the breakfast bar. Dave is standing a little behind her, looking rather nervous and uncomfortable. "Sit down, kids," my mom says, her demeanor calm in comparison. "We'd like to talk to you."

I've been anticipating this conversation. With school looming on the horizon, it would be wise to discuss how we're going to handle our new relationship with Dave. Obviously, we'll have to go back to calling him Mr. Bartley. And I'm sure he wants to instruct us to play it cool when he gives us higher marks than all our classmates.

"Dave and I have something to tell you," my mom says, glancing back at him and smiling. "We...uh..." She clears her throat. "This may come as a bit of a surprise to you both but..."

Oh my god, they're getting married! I turn my face away to stare out the darkened window, trying to hide the disturbing emotions this stirs in me. This is much more serious than I'd expected. Does that mean he'll be moving in here? Walking around in his underwear? Even if he doesn't walk around in his underwear, everyone at school will think he does. And how does one treat their algebra teacher/step-dad? I wonder if I could get them to postpone the wedding until I've graduated?

My mom continues, "We've got some very exciting news. Dave and I—" again, she turns to smile at a nervous Dave— "we're going to have a baby."

I feel the color drain from my face and I nearly topple off my seat. My mother is pregnant? She can't be. She just can't be! Why doesn't she just take out an ad in the school newspaper: *Louise Harrison's Mom Having Sex with Math Teacher.* Suddenly, I can see the appeal of wall punching.

My mom looks at me. "Are you okay?"

I'm so shocked I can barely speak. It's unbelievable that she doesn't realize how this will impact Troy and me at school. Finally I stammer, "I—I thought you were too old to get pregnant."

"Obviously I'm not," she retorts.

But what I really meant was, *You're too old to be banging my math teacher.*

"You're going to have a new little brother or sister," my mom continues, looking from Troy to me. "We weren't expecting it to happen so soon but...well..." She looks at Dave lovingly. "We're just thrilled."

Troy says, "It'll be kind of fun having a baby around here...Sort of like a puppy, but with no fur."

I could throttle him! I glance at Dave, who looks about as awkward as I did after trying to seduce Russell.

Jumping off the barstool I say, "Well, I, for one, am not thrilled. I think it's disgusting that you have to advertise your sex life to everyone in town."

"Louise..." My mom turns to Dave in exasperation. "What are you even talking about? This is a precious new life!"

"And I suppose this means he'll be moving in here and you guys will be doing it all over the place!"

"Yes, Dave's going to be living with us, but as far as 'doing it' all over the place—"

But I don't want to hear any more. "Forget it," I interrupt her, stalking to the telephone table and picking up the car keys. "I'm out of here."

"You're not taking the car, young lady," my mom says. "This conversation is not finished."

"Let her go, Denise," Dave finally speaks. "She needs some time to process all this."

Alone in the car, I fight back the tears that are threatening to obscure my vision. Rage courses through my veins, turning my cheeks red. Like it wasn't hard enough having one parent who was a sex maniac, now I've got two! The thought of my mother waddling into Red Cedars, all pregnant from having intercourse with Mr. Bartley, turns my stomach. They'll probably walk through the halls holding hands, while all the kids picture them screwing in my house. Oh god! They were screwing in my house! When? Where? Did they keep it in the bedroom or did they do it in the shower, which I use every day? On the living-room sofa, where I watch TV? Or on the dining room table, where I eat?

I will change schools and go live with my dad. The rest of them can be a happy family without me. Troy can stay there and play with his furless puppy and forget he ever had a big sister.

When I reach the end of our road, I instinctively turn left toward Russell's house. I need a friend right now, and he's the only one I feel comfortable sharing this news with. Leah would probably be supportive too, but since she had Mr. Bartley for math last year, this information might be a little disturbing to her as well.

A few minutes later, I pull the Mazda into the driveway of Russell's unassuming, two-story home. A light emanates from the living-room window and I pray that he is there. Hurrying up the concrete steps of the darkened front porch, I ring the doorbell. Moments later, Russell's stepmom, Tanya, answers.

"Is Russell here?" I ask, forcing an upbeat tone. Tanya and I have met on a few occasions. Despite her thick makeup and low-cut shirts, she seems like a very down-to-earth woman.

"Hi, hon. Sorry, he's not here right now."

A lump forms in my throat. "Do you know where he is?"

Tanya lowers her voice. "He and his dad had words again. He needed to cool off, so I let him take the Thunderbird for a drive."

"Any idea where?"

"Sorry, babe." She looks at me then, her eyes narrowed. "Are you okay? You look a little upset."

"Oh no!" I say brightly, backing away from the door. "I'm fine. I just felt like hanging out with Russell... no big deal."

Back in the car, I hurriedly reverse out of the driveway. I don't want to dissolve into tears there in the front yard and end up being invited in for tea and sympathy by Russell's stepmom. But when I'm a safe distance from his house, I pull over and rest my forehead on the steering wheel. I really need to talk to someone, but I'm not sure where to turn. And then, a sudden thought brightens my mood. I know where to find Russell.

As I drive up the winding hillside highway, I remember Russell's words. "Sometimes I come up here and just sit by myself and listen to music." He's got to be at the scenic make-out spot, blasting his techno tunes and stewing on his father's controlling tendencies. Well, just wait till he hears that my mom will soon be walking around school in a T-shirt emblazoned with *Your Math Teacher's Baby on Board*. That ought to put things into perspective for him.

I ease the car over the rutted path, the headlights casting an eerie glow on the deserted road ahead. Instinctively, I press the door lock button. This is just the kind of place where a serial killer would hang out, waiting for some horny teenagers to mutilate. A chill runs through me. Once I find Russell, I'll suggest we go talk at a Starbucks or somewhere else well-lit and secure. Entering the clearing, I immediately spot the Thunderbird and my heart surges with happiness. Parked beside it is a sporty little silver car and, in the distance, an aged station wagon. Cutting the headlights to give the other occupants some privacy, I pull into the spot next to Russell's.

Hopping out of the vehicle, I move toward the passenger window and peer inside. It takes a moment for my eyes to become accustomed to the dark, and when they do, I'm surprised to find the driver's seat empty. Then my attention is drawn to some movement in the backseat, some movement that can only be described as *writhing*. Peering into the darkness, I can just discern the outlines of two figures that appear to be...making out! Oh no! Russell isn't up here rehashing yet another argument with his father. He's here making out with that guy!

Quickly I step away from the vehicle, but it's too late. Something has alerted them to my presence—probably my face pressed up against the window. In the dark, I can just see Russell's shocked, almost frightened expression. But after a second he recognizes me. "Louise," he says, his tone a mixture of relief, confusion, and annoyance.

"Sorry," I reply, continuing to back away from the Thunderbird. "I—I didn't know..."

I have almost reached the safety of my car when the passenger door of the Thunderbird opens and a silent figure bursts out. With a hand held to his face, Russell's lover rushes over to the silver sports car and fumbles in his pocket for the keys. He's trying to hide his identity, but there is no mistaking him: the perfectly styled hair, the broad shoulders in the mint-green polo shirt, the chiseled jawline... "Oh my god," I mutter as he opens the door with a blip-blip and hops into the silver BMW. Reversing out dramatically, he speeds over the rutted path, probably doing all sorts of damage to the car's suspension.

By this time, Russell has emerged, looking rather disheveled and more than a little pissed off. "What are you doing here?" he demands.

"What am *I* doing here?" I gasp. "What are *you* doing here with Daniel Noran?"

It was a rhetorical question, of course. I know exactly what Russell was doing there with Daniel Noran. But it was just so hard to believe! Sienna's ultra-cool, ultra-popular boyfriend was secretly gay? Even in my most vicious revenge fantasies I hadn't envisioned this scenario. But despite the fact that this is perhaps the most brutal payback I could have wished upon my former friend, I don't feel anything resembling happiness. I can admit, if only to myself, that I still care about her.

Russell and I are seated on the hood of Tanya's Thunderbird now, both of us largely immersed in our own thoughts. "Wow," Russell says, staring at the faded denim covering his knees.

"Yeah," I mumble in turn.

"I knew he was confused," Russell continues, "but I didn't know he had a full-on girlfriend."

"My former best friend," I add.

He looks at me. "That's a really weird coincidence, don't you think?"

"It's totally freaky!" I cry. "I mean, all this time I was hoping something bad would happen to Sienna so she would hurt like I hurt, but not this."

"It's too much."

"It is." I am quiet for a long moment. "How did you meet him?"

"I'd seen him around the mall, and we'd had eye contact a few times. He finally came over and ordered a pizza dog, and we got to talking. We just had instant chemistry."

"Do you really like him?" From my intonation, it's obvious that I find this hard to believe.

"Yes," Russell snaps defensively. "He's a very sweet guy. He's going through a lot trying to deal with his sexuality. Maybe that's affecting the way he acts toward people."

"I'll say," I snort. "At school he acts like an arrogant a-hole."

"Obviously your former friend likes him."

"Well, she's an a-hole too."

"Yeah..." Russell continues to rest his heels on the front bumper, staring at his knees.

"So what happens now?" I ask.

"I don't know. What does happen now?"

We sit in silence for a long moment, me staring at the twinkling lights of the urban sprawl below us, Russell still focusing on his pants. Finally, Russell says, "Why'd you come up here anyway?"

In all the commotion, I had momentarily forgotten that my mother was a walking advertisement for boinking my teacher. "My mom and my algebra teacher had some big news today."

"They're getting married?"

"Worse. They're going to have a baby!"

"A baby?" Russell says, his voice instantly turning syrupy. "That's great! I love babies."

"It's not great," I grumble. "Every kid at school will know that my mom's been screwing a teacher. I'll become known as the daughter of two sex maniacs—instead of just one."

"But look at the bright side," Russell says, sounding not unlike my mother. "You're going to have a new little brother or sister. You should be excited!"

I stand up. "You don't get it."

"But a baby will be so much fun to play with."

"You'd feel differently if your dad knocked Tanya up."

"No, I wouldn't. I already know they have sex."

"Yes, but at least they're not *advertising* it! I mean, I know lots of parents have sex, but they're supposed to do it late at night, quietly, and with each other. For all my mom's and my dad's discretion, they might as well have done it right in front of me. God! My dad practically *did* do it in front of my brother! We're both going to need so much therapy."

Russell laughs. "Aren't we all?"

We hang out for a few more minutes and then I inspect my watch in the darkness. "I'd better get the car home before my mom sends out a search party."

"Yeah, I may as well go too."

Sliding off the hood I turn to face Russell. "What are you going to do about Daniel?"

"I don't know."

"You have to tell him to break up with Sienna."

"It doesn't work that way," he says, sounding a little exasperated with me. "I can't *tell* him to do anything."

"Well, obviously this can't go on!" I say.

"Okay, *Mom*," Russell snaps.

It's been ages since I've been accused of momlike behavior, and I can't deny that Russell's words sting. "Whatever," I say sullenly, heading for my mom's car.

"Yeah, whatever," he grumbles, opening the Thunderbird's door. I feel a familiar flutter of fear in my chest as I watch Russell prepare to leave. Have I handled this whole thing badly? Have I destroyed yet another friendship by being too judgmental? Have I got some kind of personality disorder that will keep me from ever having a BFF?

But before Russell closes the door he says, "I'll see you at work tomorrow. We can talk about this some more then."

𝄢

I barely sleep that night, tossing and turning over Daniel's affair with Russell, Sienna's impending heartache and humiliation, and my mother's fertile relationship with my math teacher. When morning arrives, I have come to some conclusions:

I will not interfere in the whole Russell-Daniel-Sienna triangle. I cannot risk losing my closest friend due to my maternal (read: bossy and judgmental) ways. Besides, it's not like Sienna and Daniel are going to get married or anything. And when she does ultimately get dumped and humiliated, well...she sort of deserves it.

I will steadfastly refuse to celebrate my mother's pregnancy. From this day forward, I will give her the cold shoulder to demonstrate my anger at her lack of concern for how her sexual practices affect her existing children. And I have decided to go back to calling Dave Mr. Bartley.

When I walk into the kitchen, my mom is pouring herself a cup of coffee. She calls over her shoulder to Dave, seated at the breakfast bar in front of a bowl of cereal and the paper. "Don't worry, honey, it's Swiss Water decaf. It's perfectly safe for the ba—" She stops when she sees me. "Oh, hi, honey," she says, her voice conciliatory. "Are you feeling better today?"

"Not really," I retort, grabbing a bowl from the cupboard. "Would you please pass me the cereal, Mr. Bartley?" My mom and Dave exchange amused looks, but I ignore them. Filling my bowl with Raisin Bran and milk, I return to my room to eat.

That afternoon at Orange Julius, I explain my neutral policy regarding the love triangle to Russell. "I'm sorry if I was sounding bossy and judgmental last night," I begin. "I've thought a lot about it and it wasn't right for me to tell you what to do. If you want to keep seeing Daniel behind Sienna's back . . . well, that's your decision."

He smiles at me. "Are you giving me your blessing, Mom?"

"I'm not your mom!" I shriek, drawing the attention of several food-court patrons. I lower my voice. "I'm not your mom. I'm your cool, nonjudgmental friend."

"I'm just teasing you." Russell reaches for the hot dog tongs and halfheartedly turns a few dogs. "I don't know what I'm going to do about Daniel, but it's not as simple as telling him to break up with Sienna."

"It's not?"

"If he chooses me over her, that's like admitting he's gay, and he's not ready to do that. His parents put a lot of pressure on him to go to college, join his dad's fraternity, and eventually his law firm. They want him to marry a nice girl and have some nice little grandchildren. When—or *if* he comes out, it could change his whole life."

"But he can't just live a lie!" I say rather desperately. For the first time ever, I feel something less than distaste for Daniel Noran. It's bizarre, but what I feel for him right now borders on pity.

Russell puts a hot dog in a bun and slathers it with mustard. "It takes a lot to be a gay man in a straight man's world," he says, sounding about forty instead of seventeen. "A lot of guys don't have the guts. It's sad, but it's true."

My problems suddenly seem ridiculously small. "I'm definitely going to stay out of it from now on," I say, handing him a paper napkin to catch a drip of mustard. "This is *way* too complicated for me."

The last few days of my summer vacation are relatively calm. This is not to say that I'm not still bothered by recent events. Ever since my mom's announcement, it's like she's suddenly blossomed into this round, glowing pregnant creature. She's always saying annoying things, like "I can't believe I'm showing so much already. I guess all my abdominal muscles are stretched out from carrying Louise and Troy" and "I hope this baby's head isn't as big as Louise's was. I thought she was going to split me in two!"

Before school starts, Dave sits Troy and me down in the living room. Obviously, he doesn't need to tell me to call him Mr. Bartley at school, since I've already reverted to that formal title—when I remember, of course.

"Well...school's almost back in session," he says.

"Yeah, we know," I mumble.

"I don't want you kids to feel uncomfortable about my relationship with your mom."

"Too late," I growl.

Dave sighs. "Louise, I know you're not thrilled about it, but your mother and I are together and we're going to stay together, so you may as well accept it."

I know he's right, but I still feel they deserve to be punished with my hostility for causing me such embarrassment. I shrug mutely and stare at the coffee table.

Mr. Bartley continues. "Now that I'm living here, I thought it would be too awkward for you to be in my class this year, so I've arranged for you both to have other math teachers."

"Darn," Troy says, "I thought I'd get an A for once."

"Sorry, my friend," Dave replies, "I guess you're going to have to earn it." He looks to me.

"What?" I snap. "That's fine. It's not like I *loved* your algebra class so much last year."

"Okay then," Dave says, clapping his hands on his legs and standing up. "I'm glad that's all sorted out."

At least things with Russell and me are still solid. I have stuck to my vow not to interfere in his relationship with Daniel Noran—if *relationship* is the right word for something so volatile. "It's over," Russell says over Mocha Frappuccinos at Starbucks. "He says he was just experimenting. He wants to make things work with Sienna."

I put my hand on his. "Are you okay?"

"Yeah...It was just a bit of fun." But I can hear the sadness in his voice. He looks at me and brightens. "We'll be in New York soon anyway."

"Only one more year to go and we're out of here!"

"Let's focus on the future!"

"Definitely," I say. "I'm going to devote this year to getting my portfolio ready for art school."

"And I'm going to send out a bunch of sample CDs to New York City clubs."

But on Labor Day weekend, things have changed yet again. We're working a Saturday shift when Russell casually says, "I saw Daniel last night."

I whirl around from the Wild Blue Twist I'm blending. "You did?"

"Yeah." He waits for me to serve my customer before continuing. "He really misses me and he's going to end things with Sienna."

"What?" I know I'm supposed to be cool and nonjudgmental about this, but I can't believe Daniel is playing Russell and Sienna this way. "Last week he said you were just an experiment."

Russell laughs. "He didn't say *I* was an experiment, he said he was *experimenting*."

"So he's going to break up with Sienna then?"

"When the timing's right," he says. "He doesn't want to hurt her too much."

But as soon as I walk through the doors of Red Cedars on September 5, I am met by the sound of Sienna's ringing laughter. That's definitely not the sound of a girl whose boyfriend has just dropped her for a guy. As I pass through the lobby, I glance over at her clique occupying their usual space at the bottom of the stairwell. Kimber and Jessie are there, of course, as are Liam and Aidan, two slick, good-looking guys. And holding court at the center of the group are Sienna and Daniel. Sienna is seated on the bottom stair and Daniel is one above her, his arms draped possessively over her shoulders. For only the briefest moment, I experience that old sense of alienation, but I shake it off. I'm almost through the lobby and entering the hallway when Daniel looks up. It's the first time Daniel Noran and I have had eye contact. In fact, it could be the first time he's ever looked at me. But in his blue eyes I don't see the cool arrogance I'd expected. There is a pleading desperation in them. Quickly, I look away.

Leah Montgomery and Emma Johnston find me on the way to homeroom. "Can you believe this is our last year here?" Emma says, a wistful twinge to her voice.

"Thank god!" I say, and they both laugh.

Leah says, "Did you hear about Aaron Hansen?"

"No, what?"

"He spent the summer interning with this theater group in Chicago. He's staying there for three more weeks."

"Cool."

"What about you?" Emma asks me. "Anything exciting happen in your life this summer?"

Oh . . . well, my mom got knocked up by our algebra teacher and I discovered that the most popular guy in school is secretly gay. I don't actually say this, of course. Instead I shrug and say, "Not really . . . I mostly just worked and hung out with Russell."

"You're lucky!" Emma gushes. "He's so gorgeous!"

"I know," I say a little ruefully.

"Speaking of gorgeous," Leah says, "there's Red Cedar's golden couple." Sienna and Daniel are approaching hand in hand. Something about her self-satisfied smile and his ultra-confident swagger irks me. If the rest of the school knew what I know, they wouldn't look so smug.

"You know he's gay, don't you?" I say loudly.

Leah and Emma look at me. Out of the corner of my eye, I can feel Daniel's attention on me as well. "Russell," I explain. "He's gay."

"I knew," Leah says.

"Yeah, I kind of figured," Emma seconds.

"Well, you know what they say," I continue with a loud laugh. "If a guy is too good-looking and too well-dressed, he's probably gay!" I have no idea if this is truly what they say, but it certainly applies to both Russell and Daniel. At that moment, the second bell rings and we all hurry toward our homerooms. Daniel and Sienna pass by me without a glance, but something in his tense posture tells me that I've gotten to him.

After school, I call Russell. "Daniel hasn't broken up with Sienna yet."

"He will," he replies confidently. "He's just waiting for the right time."

"But when will it be the right time?" I demand. "When they've been together for six months? A year? When they've been voted best-looking and most popular couple ever in the history of Red Cedars?"

"I thought you were going to stay out of this?" he says, an edge to his voice.

He's right; I thought I was, but I didn't realize it would be so hard! "You don't know what it's like to see them together. They walk around like they're the king and queen of the school, and it's all just a lie."

Russell's voice is quiet when he finally answers. "Yeah...that would be pretty hard to watch."

And finally, I clue in. Sure, it's irritating for me to watch Daniel and Sienna together, but the situation is downright painful for Russell. "I'm really gonna try to stay out of it from now on," I promise.

"Thanks. I think that would be best."

"It's not going to be easy though."

"It won't be for much longer," Russell assures me. "He's going to end it with her soon."

While his voice sounds optimistic, I can't help but pick up a hint of doubt.

It's not easy, but I do a pretty good job of sticking to my policy of noninterference. When I see Sienna and her Prince Charming in the hallway, I force myself to turn away in case I make some comment about living a lie or kissing gay frogs. If Russell can put his trust in Daniel to do the right thing, then so can I. And whenever Sienna's smug happiness becomes a little hard to take, I remind myself that she's about to be devastated by her boyfriend's confession of homosexuality. Instead of finding her annoying, I will pity her. Given the years of friendship in our past, it's the least I can do.

The only positive aspect of my obsession with their love triangle is that it has distracted me from my mom's relationship with Mr. Bartley. On the few occasions when I've passed Dave in the hallway, I've simply muttered a casual "hey," instead of screaming and fleeing in the other direction. In fact, I'm feeling largely unconcerned about that aspect of my life. Compared to the Daniel Noran situation, the fact that my mother is about to become Mr. Bartley's baby momma doesn't seem that big a deal.

That is, until Thursday at lunchtime, when, without any warning, my worst fear is realized. A few of us are leaning against Leah's locker talking when she appears in the distance. She's walking down the hall—or should I say *waddling* down the hall, her enormously round stomach leading the way to Mr. Bartley's classroom. Okay, my mom isn't really *that* big, but that belly of hers is obviously more than just beer and pizza. My first instinct is to make a loud noise or crack a joke or something—anything to keep my friends focused on me and not the obviously pregnant form of my mother lumbering to the math room. But if I do create some kind of outburst, will it attract my mom's attention? Will she come over and say, "Hi, honey! Hi, girls! Would you like to touch my stomach and feel the child I created from your math teacher's seed?"

It appears there's nothing I can do but stare mutely in her direction. I am paralyzed with fear at our secret being discovered. No one even knows my mom and Mr. Bartley are dating, let alone that he has impregnated her—in my own house, quite possibly on my dining-room table! As she enters the math class, I breathe a sigh of relief, but it is premature. Emma Johnston says, "Hey, Louise. Wasn't that your mom?"

"Uh..." My face instantly turns beet red. "I didn't notice."

"Is she pregnant?" Raj Sohota asks.

I clear my throat nervously. "Umm...yeah."

Leah says, "I thought your parents were split up?"

"They are." Right on cue, my mom and Mr. Bartley exit his classroom. He is carrying her, her legs wrapped around his waist and they are necking furiously. Okay, they're just walking side by side, but with the intimate laughter they're sharing, they might as well be.

Emma mumbles, "Oh..." And we all stand there silently as my mom and her lover move toward the exit. I want to disappear, to dissolve into a pile of salt. This is too humiliating to live through! But they're almost gone. If I can just endure the next few seconds, my mom and Dave will have left the building. I'll swear Emma, Leah, and Raj to secrecy, and when I get home tonight, I'll talk to my mom about waiting for Mr. Bartley in the car from now on.

But just as my mom and Dave reach the end of the hallway, the exit door opens and Kimber and Jessie walk through. Oh god! Of the six hundred students at Red Cedars, why does it have to be these two? Their scintillating conversation about liquid versus pressed-powder foundation stops abruptly when they spot the rotund woman accompanying Mr. Bartley. "Hi, Ms. Burroughs," Kimber says. "Hi, Mr. Bartley."

"Hello, girls," my mom and Dave answer, completely oblivious to the malicious tone in Kimber's voice. They walk out into the warm autumn sunshine, unaware of the emotional devastation they have left in their wake.

Kimber and Jessie continue toward us, looking over their shoulders and giggling cruelly. When they're a few lockers away, Jessie says, "Louise, why didn't you tell us your mom got knocked up by Mr. Bartley? That's so... *weird*."

Before I can reply that I know it's weird and I wish it had never happened and there's no need to tell me that both my parents are sex maniacs because I am all too aware, Leah says, "I think it's exciting. It'll be so much fun to have a new baby around."

"Totally," Raj agrees, "I love babies."

Emma jumps in. "Me too. And this way, you'll get all the fun, but you can just hand it off to your mom when it cries or poops or something."

A swell of intense gratitude fills me and I smile weakly at my three friends. But of course, Kimber and Jessie are not swayed. "Whatevs!" Kimber says with an incredulous laugh. They walk off, their mocking laughter ringing in my ears. I watch them for a moment as they gleefully spread the news to passersby that my so-called normal parent has been screwing a teacher.

At home that night, I approach my mom in the kitchen, where she is assembling zucchini lasagna. "I'm dropping out of school," I say. "I'm going to get my GED and I'm moving to New York with Russell."

"What's brought all this on?"

"Like you don't know." I open the fridge and peer inside.

My mom puts down the block of cheese she's grating. "No, I don't know. Why don't you enlighten me?"

I turn to face her. "I saw you waddling around the school today, practically making out with Mr. Bartley in front of everyone!"

"Louise! I did no such thing!"

"I didn't want anyone to know you were pregnant!" I cry. "Why couldn't you have had some respect for me and waited for him in the car?"

My mom is flabbergasted. "I—We were just going for lunch. I...Shut the fridge door."

I do. "There's nothing good in there anymore anyway. It's all healthy stuff *for the baby*."

She looks at me then and I can tell she's fed up. "Do you know how juvenile you're being about this?"

"Whatever. I have to get ready for work."

"You think you're mature enough to quit school and move to a city like New York on your own? You're not mature enough to handle the fact that sometimes adults fall in love, and yes, they have sex, and yes, that's how babies are made."

"STOP!"

"It's not a healthy attitude, Louise. You're going to have to learn to deal with this pregnancy. I'm not going to hide myself away to save you the embarrassment."

"Of course not!" I yell. "Who cares about your oldest child? You've got Dave and your precious new baby to think about. You can just forget about me!" I stomp from the kitchen and into my room, slamming the door behind me. I have to admit that this does little to refute my mom's "juvenile" comment, but at that moment, it just feels so right.

The fight with my mom is the catalyst I needed to make me cement my plans for the future. When I get to work, I talk to Russell about it. "So, who do I call to take the GED?"

He appears surprised. "Why? What happened?" When I describe the earlier hallway encounter, Russell's voice registers his concern. "Oh, shit."

"Yeah, so obviously I can't go back there. I need to take that test so we can move to New York."

"Well, I took it in Phoenix, so I don't really know. I guess you could just google GED Langley or something."

"I'll do it as soon as I get home."

Russell leans against the counter and looks at me. "But are you really ready to go to New York *now*? I mean, I'm going to need almost a year to save up enough money, and I haven't even contacted any clubs yet. And what about your portfolio?"

I am immediately suspicious. "What? Don't you want to go now?"

"Of course I do! I just don't think there's a huge rush."

"Fine. Sure, whatever," I grumble.

I try not to read too much into his hesitance, but I can't help but worry. I want to get out of Langley more than ever, and Russell seems almost indifferent. But it's a busy night, so we have little opportunity to debate the subject. In fact, we work our shift in virtual silence, perfunctorily serving customers and basically ignoring each other. It's not until Russell is cashing out that I extend the olive branch.

"My mom let me drive tonight," I say. "Do you want a ride home?"

"That's okay," he responds. "Tanya's picking me up."

"*Tanya* is?"

"Yes," he snaps, looking at me with narrowed eyes. "*Tanya* is."

"Okay... well, everything else is done but the cash so... I guess I'll take off."

Without looking up from the float he says, "See ya later."

As I walk to my mom's car in the darkened parking lot, I feel fairly sure that Tanya is not the one coming to fetch Russell. Daniel Noran has undoubtedly told Sienna he is busy doing something macho like getting a tattoo or crocodile wrestling as an excuse to meet up with his boyfriend. Scanning the nearly deserted parking lot, I don't see Tanya's large blue Thunderbird entering the dimly lit area. In fact, other than my mom's Mazda and the steel-grey Mercedes parked next to it, it's practically vacant.

Pressing the automatic unlocking device, I see the car's headlights blink to welcome me. I have just reached the driver's side door when I suddenly sense the unmistakable presence of another person. Instantly, my heart leaps into my throat and my mother's numerous warnings about staying alert and aware of your surroundings when alone in a dark area run through my head. Damn Russell, Sienna, and Daniel! Damn my mom, Mr. Bartley, and the evil triplets! How am I supposed to stay alert and aware of my surroundings when I've got so much on my mind? My blood will be on their hands when I am raped and murdered by the Willowbrook Mall parking-lot killer!

That's when he emerges from the Mercedes parked on the passenger side of my car. "Hi," he says cheerfully, smiling that broad, white-toothed smile.

There is a moment of relief, followed by a resurgence of fear. Sure, Daniel Noran is less likely to be a parking-lot serial killer, but that doesn't mean he wouldn't like to see me dead.

He continues, "You're Louise Harrison, right?"

Right, I'm tempted to snap. *We've only gone to school together for four years. I'm the best friend of your boyfriend and the former best friend of your girlfriend, but how could I expect someone like you to know my name?* But it's probably best not to antagonize him. "Yeah," I reply.

"So...uh." He's still smiling, "I think you already know who I am."

"Yep."

"I was wondering if we could talk."

"About what?" I say nervously.

"I think you already know that too."

"Well...okay. But my mom is expecting me home soon."

"It won't take too long," Daniel says, friendly manner still in place. He motions to the Mercedes. "Do you want to get in? It's my mom's car. It's got a great stereo."

Never get into a car with someone who would like to see you dead, I vaguely remember hearing. "No, we can talk here."

"Okay." For the first time, Daniel's composure seems to slip a little. He takes a deep, labored breath before continuing. "So, uh...I know you saw Russell and me together."

"Yeah."

"And you used to be really good friends with Sienna, right?"

"*Used* to."

"I just wanted to tell you that I'm not trying to play games here. I'm sure this must seem really awful..."

"It does." This may very well prompt him to attack, but I simply can't deny this fact.

"I know, I know," he says, running his fingers through his ridiculously perfect hair. "But it's complicated. My parents, they expect a lot from me. My dad—"

I cut him off. "Russell told me."

He looks at me intently then. "You seem like a really smart person, Louise. I'm sure you can understand how complex this situation is. It's not as simple as just choosing between Russell and Sienna."

I shrug.

Daniel pauses and then flashes me another devastating smile. "I hear you're a really great artist too."

"Uh, thanks." Almost against my will, I can feel myself softening toward him. Am I really that gullible? Or is Daniel Noran really that charming?

"I saw your sets for *Rent*. I could totally see you ending up on Broadway one day."

He *is* that charming! But I can't forget what he's doing to my former and current best friends. "What do you want from me, Daniel?"

Again, his hands run through his thick, dark hair. "Please, just give me a chance to make things right. I don't want to hurt Sienna. She's a really great girl and...well, it would be really painful for her if you told her about...well, you know."

I nod my understanding.

"Not to mention that she won't believe you anyway. She'll think you're just trying to hurt her and she'll be angry. You don't deserve to go through that."

Daniel is giving me an almost pitying look that makes me shift uncomfortably on my feet. Unfortunately, his prediction of Sienna's reaction sounds pretty accurate.

He coughs nervously into his hand. "I know I'm going to have to tell my parents and my friends...It's not going to be easy, but...it's something I have to do."

"It is," I say gently. And then, to show him how empathetic I am, I say, "Did you see *Brokeback Mountain*? I just thought it was so sad how those cowboys had to live a lie their entire lives."

He gives me kind of a strange look. "Uh...yeah. So, you'll leave it with me then? You'll let me end things with Sienna?"

"Okay, but you'd better do it soon. It's not going to get any easier."

"I know." He pauses for a second. "If it makes you feel any better, we're not...uh, doing anything *physical*, if you know what I mean."

This does make me feel a little better. Maybe Sienna isn't that serious about him after all?

Daniel continues, "I guess that old guy she was dating pressured her a lot. When we hooked up, she told me she didn't want to rush things. And, uh...that was fine by me."

Daniel doesn't want to have sex with the most gorgeous girl at Red Cedars and he's *confused* about his sexuality? "Okay," I say, "I won't say anything to Sienna."

His relief is obvious. "Thanks, Louise. You really are a great person, just like Russell and Sienna said."

I look at him. "Sienna said?"

"Yeah," he flashes his brilliant white smile, "she has a lot of nice things to say about you. Your dad, on the other hand..."

A sick feeling rises in my stomach. "Right. Okay, well, good luck breaking up with her and...coming out and everything."

"Thanks," he says, still standing outside his mom's Mercedes. He watches me hop into the driver's seat and tear out of the parking lot.

Because of my late-night encounter with Daniel Noran, I had nearly forgotten about my mom's display of her fertility in the Red Cedars hallways yesterday. But as soon as I walk into the foyer, it all comes flooding back. As I hurry toward my locker, I can't help but notice the halted conversations, hear the excited whispers, and feel the eyes upon me. Maybe if I keep my head down and don't make eye contact, no one will comment on my mom's sexual relationship with Mr. Bartley? But the buzz of conversation lets me know that's unlikely. I'm undoing my combination lock when she approaches.

"Hey, Louise," Kimber says casually.

"Uh...hey." There is a brief moment of hope. Maybe Kimber doesn't think it's such a big deal that my mom is pregnant with Mr. Bartley's love child? And that's when I notice it. Kimber has tucked a sweater or a backpack or something else enormous under her shirt and is waddling up and down the hallway. Jessie, Audrey, and a gaggle of popular girls and guys are laughing hysterically into their palms. I turn back to my locker, my cheeks burning with shame.

But apparently Audrey doesn't think this humiliation is sufficient. She approaches. "So, I hear your mom and Mr. Bartley are a couple?" I mumble an unintelligible affirmation. Audrey looks back at the peanut gallery and then continues. "We were all wondering, like, do you ever hear them having sex at night? I've been to your house before. Your bedroom is just across the hall from your mom's. You must hear them going at it sometimes."

"No."

"Have you ever walked in on them while they're doing it?" she continues excitedly. "I bet you've come home from work and found them having sex on the sofa! Or the kitchen table!" Audrey's cohorts burst into uproarious laughter. Normally, this would cause me to crawl into my locker and shut the door—not that someone my size could ever fit into a locker—but something is different today. Maybe I'm PMSing, but I have had enough. I whirl on her.

"Sure," I say, my voice dripping with sarcasm. "My mom and Mr. Bartley have sex all over the house! I've probably seen them do it at least thirty times."

Audrey looks to the group behind her. "She admits it!" she cries delightedly.

"Oh yeah," I continue, my volume increasing. "They actually put on sex shows for us! Every night! They're total perverts. My whole family is! You should know that by now." To emphasize my point, I slam my locker door. Audrey just looks at me. There are a few awkward giggles, but my outburst has definitely quelled their hysterics. I want nothing more than to run to the bathroom and burst into tears, but

I will not give them the satisfaction. I hold my ground, staring at Audrey with angry eyes.

"God," Audrey finally says, "what a biatch! I was just asking—"

But from somewhere within the circle of onlookers, a voice interrupts. "Shut up, Audrey."

I look to see who on earth would be brave enough to defend me in this situation and my eyes fall upon Sienna. Audrey is as shocked as I am. "What?" she says, laughing awkwardly.

"I said shut up," Sienna continues. "Her mom's having a baby. Why do you have to turn it into something gross?"

Audrey looks around the circle for support. "Uh, maybe because it *is* gross! Her mom is, like, doing Mr. Bartley."

"So?" Sienna says, walking toward her. "Why are you so interested? Do you have a crush on him or something?"

"No!" Audrey shrieks as the onlookers stifle their giggles.

"Well, then why do you care what he does with Louise's mom?"

Audrey is about to make a bitchy retort, but she knows better than to go up against Sienna. "I don't, obviously." She laughs again, stepping away from me a little. "Like...whatever."

I take this opportunity to flee to homeroom.

6

As predicted, I am the topic of numerous whispered conversations for the rest of the day. They're probably all talking about how the humiliation of being the daughter of two sex-crazed parents has caused me to snap, firing back at one of the most popular girls in school. Leah, Emma, and the gang try to be supportive, but there's really nothing they can say to help. At least no one is outwardly attacking me anymore. They're all too afraid that I'll pull out a hand grenade and blow us all to smithereens.

After fourth period, I allow myself a break. I've kept on a brave, almost defiant face all day, and I can feel the mask starting to slip. When English Lit is over, I slip into the bath-room and secure myself in a stall. It's not like I feel the need to cry anymore, I just feel exhausted. Sitting on the edge of the toilet seat, I wearily drop my head into my hands.

I'm not sure how long I stay like that. Fifth period is calculus, so there seems no good reason to emerge. It isn't until I realize that the time I'm wasting hiding in a toilet stall could be used researching the GED angle that I decide to come out. Blowing my nose loudly, I flush the toilet and head to the row of sinks. Washing my hands, I take in my reflection in the long, rectangular mirror. The day's trauma is weighing heavily on my appearance. My nose looks red and shiny and there are dark circles under my watery eyes. But what does it matter? Once I take the equivalency test, I can leave this school and reinvent myself in New York.

Just as I'm turning to leave, she enters. I stop in my tracks. It's kind of surprising that this has never happened before— Sienna and me, face-to-face in a secluded, private setting. Sienna jumps a little, obviously shocked to see me as well. While I feel infinitely too exhausted to speak to my for-mer BFF right now, I guess a thank-you for coming to my defense is in order.

"Uh...thanks, you know...for before," I mumble.

"Right," she says, and her tone is dismissive. "It was no big deal." Sienna heads into a bathroom stall and I prepare to leave. I have just turned the corner when I hear her say, "I just think it's sick, that's all."

Somewhat hesitantly, I turn back. "What?" I ask, my heart in my throat.

Sienna steps out of the stall. "The way Audrey and Kimber and those guys were acting. I mean, it's kind of weird to turn happy news about a baby into something about sex. But you know them"—she rolls her eyes—"they're total sex maniacs."

Surprisingly, she doesn't follow this with "like your dad." I shrug and give a small snort of affirmation.

"So...Mr. Bartley lives with you guys now?"

I nod.

"I think..." she begins, suddenly sounding nervous, "that's nice...Your mom deserves to be happy after...everything."

I just nod again, my eyes beginning to pool with tears. I want to say something to her, something like: *I want you to know that I'll always be there for you too—like, if something horrible were to happen between you and Daniel, you can count on me.* But I'm too afraid to speak. Instead, I bite my lip to stifle a sob and shrug. Sensing the impending breakdown, Sienna says, "Well...congratulations on your new brother or sister," and closes herself back into the stall.

I skip calculus and head home. As I walk, I let the tears pour unchecked down my cheeks. The exchange with Sienna today confirmed what I had thought: all the years of friendship between us can't just be forgotten. We will always care about each other. This makes the fact that we will never be friends again that much harder to take. And this makes me miss Sienna even more.

Letting myself in to our empty house, I'm met by a comforting silence. My mom is at work, and Dave and Troy are still at school. I wander into the kitchen and rifle through the cupboards. This is the kind of moment that calls for a martini, but since I don't know what's in a martini and even if I did, I certainly wouldn't find the ingredients in my pregnant mother's house, I settle for a glass of iced tea. Taking my drink into the living room, I sink into the sofa. But before I've even had a sip, I fall into an exhausted sleep.

I'm awakened by my brother's noisy entrance. "You're *sleeping*?" he says, like he's just walked in on me rubbing peanut butter in my hair. "It's, like, quarter to five."

"I was tired," I grumble, sitting up groggily. I go to the bathroom to splash some water on my face and rub the sleep out of my eyes. When I emerge, my mom and Dave are both home. They're in the kitchen, putting away some groceries.

"Hi," my mom says gently, coming over to me. "Troy said you were asleep when he came in. Are you feeling okay?"

"Yeah," I say, "just tired."

She puts her hand on my forehead. "You're not warm..."

I suddenly feel like crying again. Damn! I thought I'd gotten it all out of my system. For a fleeting moment, I consider opening up to my mom about the day's events but decide that it might be a little cruel to tell her about the taunting I've endured because of her pregnancy. Instead, I remove her hand from my head and give it a squeeze. "I'm okay," I say. "Everything's okay."

My mom's chin quivers with emotion, and she pulls me to her for a tight hug. "I love you, you know," she whispers into my hair. "You'll always be my first baby."

"I know," I say back. "I love you too."

When school resumes on Monday, life has taken on an almost eerie normalcy. No one mentions the fact that my mom is having Mr. Bartley's baby. After all the cruel teasing and Kimber's pregnancy imitations, it's almost like no one really cares. For the next few days, I spend my time with Leah and the girls, once again completely ignored by the evil triplets. And neither Sienna nor Daniel acknowledges the momentous exchanges that occurred between us the previous week.

Of course, I try to ignore them in turn. I immerse myself in school, work, and my art portfolio, but I can't deny that secretly I am still watching, waiting for Daniel to make good on his promise. But Sienna's smiling face and confident manner are certainly not that of a girl who's just discovered her boyfriend's gay.

But when I walk into the cafeteria at Wednesday lunchtime, something has changed. Sienna's table of popular girls is positively abuzz, their words and actions as frenetic as a beehive. Well... there can be only one explanation. Daniel's finally done it. I feel a mix of emotions as I observe the swarm of girls surrounding Sienna, obscuring her from my vision.

While Daniel's confession today will save her infinitely more heartache in the long run, I know firsthand how hard it is to find out that the man you love is gay. And as much as I despise Sienna's friends, I'm glad she has them right now.

"Hey," Raj says as I join her, Emma, and Leah. She motions her head toward Sienna's table. "Did you hear the news?"

"Uh, sort of," I say modestly, not wanting to let on that I was instrumental in the events that played out today.

Emma rolls her eyes. "Can you believe it? A promise ring! That's so . . . *fifties*."

"Sorry, what?" I gasp.

"Daniel Noran gave Sienna Marshall a promise ring," Raj explains.

Leah looks at me. "Why? What did you think it was?"

"I—I thought I heard something else," I stammer. "It . . . doesn't matter."

"So, I guess they're all celebrating," Emma continues, staring at the gaggle of girls.

Now that I listen more carefully, there is definitely a celebratory vibe at their table. I manage to catch a glimpse of Sienna through the throng. Her face is beaming as she holds forth her hand to her numerous admirers.

Raj takes a bite of her sandwich, then mumbles, "What does a promise ring even mean these days?"

"I promise to marry you one day in ten years or something," Leah says. "It's, like, prehistoric."

Emma elaborates. "Supposedly, it's a promise to wait for each other until after college. It's like a pre-engagement ring."

I stand up. "I've got to go."

The girls look at me. Leah says, "Are you okay? You didn't even eat anything."

"I'm fine," I say, forcing a smile. "I've got to go...talk to Mr. Bartley. Yeah, my mom asked me to tell him something and I almost forgot." Gathering my lunch bag, I hurriedly exit the room.

In the hallway, I begin a frantic search for Daniel Noran. How could he betray me this way? Okay, it probably wasn't too hard for him to betray *me*, since he barely knows my name, but how could he betray Russell this way? And how could he dupe Sienna? Obviously, she and I are not as close as we once were, but I can't stand by and watch her get pre-engaged to someone so deceitful, so duplicitous, not to mention so gay!

And then I spot him. He's at the far end of one of the hallways, surrounded by a group of cool, popular guys. They're an intimidating bunch, with their expensive clothes and their superior laughter, but I force myself to move toward them. If I hesitate, I may chicken out.

Jake Lawrence is saying, "God, I can't believe you did it! Like, why, man? You're only eighteen!"

"I know why!" Aidan Kemper cries. "Some girls won't put out unless they've got a ring on their finger."

Daniel laughs. "You got me, buddy!"

"That's not why you gave Sienna a promise ring," I say. "Is it, Daniel?"

The five boys turn to look at me, their expressions relaying their shock. Most of them are stunned I'm even daring to speak to them—me, Miss Big-Boned Loser, Miss Drama

Nerd, Miss Invisible. Only Daniel's face registers recognition—and fear.

Jake laughs first. "Can we help you with something?"

"Maybe Daniel can," I say, my tone formidable.

"Hey," Liam Nordell says, "you're the chick whose mom got knocked up by Bartley!"

"Yeah," I say, addressing him, "that's me. I'm also the one whose brother walked in on Sienna's mom giving my dad a fortieth-birthday blow job. Sienna and I used to be really close, but since all that went down, not so much."

Liam gapes at me like this is the weirdest thing he's ever heard—which it just might be.

Daniel steps forward. "Give us a minute, you guys." His voice is commanding, and his entourage wanders off down the hall.

"A promise ring?" I ask, my voice hushed but frantic. "You were supposed to break up with her!"

"Yeah," he says ruefully, "there was a change of plans."

"Change of plans? You go from planning to break up with her to giving her a promise ring? What? You're suddenly straight again?"

"It's not that," he says, glancing nervously around the deserted hallway. "It's my parents. My mom's having some health problems and it's really not a good time to upset her." His hand travels through his perfect coif. "I just couldn't break her heart right now, and she really likes Sienna." He looks at me, his face full of concern. "I know you've gone through a lot with your family too. If anyone can understand, it's you, Louise."

I start to say something like, True, I do know what it's like to have to make sacrifices for your parents' happiness, but then I pause. Looking at Daniel Noran again, I notice that he's wearing that same charming, toothy smile that won me over in the parking lot last week. And that's when I know. Daniel is just one of those people for whom everything will always turn out all right. Everyone will always want to please him. Everyone will always accept his excuses. Everyone will always know his name.

"Well..." I say, my shoulders sagging with defeat, "I guess you know what you're doing."

He reaches out and gives my arm a squeeze. "I knew you'd understand."

I'm embarrassed to admit that I hope someone has witnessed this intimate exchange between me and the reigning king of Red Cedars.

"I'm going to take care of it," he says, "when the time is right."

"Okay." I take a step back. "Well, I hope your mom's okay and...see ya later."

Charming, toothy smile: "See you around, Louise."

So there's no point in me interfering. It's not like any-one would thank me for it. Russell certainly wouldn't say, *Oh, thanks, Louise. It's so nice of you to tell me that the guy I'm crazy about, the hottest, sexiest, and quite possibly* only *gay guy in Langley (Mr. Sumner notwithstanding), is a lying, manipulative dirtbag.* And I highly doubt Sienna would say, *What? My pre-fiancé is homosexual? Gee, thanks for telling me that, Louise, and saving me from a life of deception and ultimate humiliation.* Besides, Daniel could probably charm Russell into turning against me, and Sienna would definitely think I was lying just to hurt her. She'd undoubtedly instruct her followers to torture me about my parents' out-of-control sex lives at every opportunity.

After school, I call Russell. It's tempting to spill the whole sordid story to him, but I can't hurt him that way. I love him too much. And it must be hard to be gay in a back-ward suburb like ours. Not to mention that Daniel seems to have the ability to charm the pants off everyone (literally in some cases).

"So how was life at Red Cedars today?" Russell asks.

"Oh, same old thing," I lie. "How are your demo CDs coming along?"

"Good," he replies, rather unconvincingly. "My dad's been making me do a bunch of yard work, so I haven't had a lot of free time, but I'm going to get to them soon."

"You have to!" My voice is full of panic. "It's only a few months until we leave for New York!"

Russell laughs. "Yeah, it's only ten short months away."

"I'm serious. We *are* moving to New York, right? One hundred percent for sure?"

"Yes, Louise," he says, and I can picture him rolling his eyes on the other end of the phone. "We *are* moving to New York, one hundred percent for sure. We're going to get an apartment together. I'm going to get work in clubs, and you're going to go to art school."

"Okay," I say weakly.

"Will you please stop worrying about it?" His voice is caring. "Nothing is going to change our plans. I promise."

Russell's assurance makes it slightly easier to ignore Sienna and Daniel the next day as they walk through the school hallways, their fawning admirers throwing rose petals and confetti at them. God, the way Audrey, Jessie, and Kimber are carrying on, you'd think this was the wedding of some huge celebrities or something.

I try to tune them out, but unfortunately the evil triplets are in my history class and sit only a few seats up from me. While we wait for Ms. Harmon's arrival, they babble on about Sienna's nuptials like they're happening next week.

"Of course you'll be my bridesmaids!" Sienna assures them, prompting a delighted squeal from Kimber and a slightly tearful hug from Audrey.

"So, where do you think you'll get married?" Kimber says.

"Well, not in Langley, that's for sure!" Sienna laughs. "I mean, who knows where we'll end up. Daniel's dad's got him a mailroom job at this really great law firm in New York City for the summer..."

My head jerks up from the paper I've been doodling on.

Sienna continues, "And then he'll go to Cornell, so, we'll definitely be on the East Coast. Daniel knows I've always wanted to live in New York City, and his dad has lots of connections there."

A wave of nausea overtakes me as I blatantly stare at Sienna and her friends. Daniel is going to be in New York this summer! He and Sienna are going to move there one day! So, he could carry on his relationships with Russell and Sienna indefinitely!

Just then, Sienna feels my gaze upon her. She looks in my direction and our eyes meet. She gives me a small, tentative smile.

Much to my dismay, I feel my eyes begin to well with tears, yet again. I look away and begin to rifle through the largely empty pages of my notebook. God, I can't break down in front of everyone. I've got to get out of here. Unfortunately, just as I'm about to flee, Ms. Harmon enters the room and closes the door behind her.

I sit through history class in a sort of daze. In fact, I sit through all my classes in a fog. With this new information, everything has suddenly changed. Well, not *everything* has changed. I'm still completely powerless. There's still nothing I can do.

When school is finally over, I gratefully make my way home. Tonight I have a five o'clock shift at Orange Julius with Russell. Normally, this would be the highlight of my day, but I just can't face him tonight. Going to the phone, I dial Grant's cell phone. "I'm really sick," I weakly tell his voice mail. "I've got some serious cramps and I won't be able to work tonight." Something tells me this particular excuse will work on Grant.

When my mom gets home, I'm lying on the couch watching *Oprah*. "I thought you had to work tonight?" she says, dropping her purse on the floor at the end of the couch.

"No," I lie, "I thought I did, but I was looking at next week's schedule." I can safely assume that my mom would be even stricter about missing work than she is about missing school.

"Well, that's nice," she says, coming to sit beside me. She lifts my feet up and places them on her lap. Looking at the TV she says, "So what's going on here?"

"This woman's trying to get back on her feet after her husband left her," I mumble.

"Bastard," she says.

Whether it's my mom's proximity or the poor woman on TV, I feel a return of the emotion that nearly overwhelmed me earlier today. Biting my lip, I stifle the urge to confess all to my mother. Knowing her, she would instantly call a meeting of everyone's parents, throwing in the school counselor, principal, and a few extra teachers for good measure. Needless to say, this would cement my position as the twelfth grade's biggest loser.

"What's for dinner?" I ask in an attempt to distract myself from an emotional breakdown. Food often works well in these cases.

"I've got some ground turkey in the fridge. I thought I'd make chili or something."

"I'll do it," I say, lifting my feet from her lap and placing them on the floor. "You stay here and watch TV."

"Thanks, honey." My mom smiles up at me. "I am pretty tired. But now that I'm in my second trimester, I should have more energy soon."

"It's okay."

She looks at me lovingly. "You're a good girl, Louise."

Oh no! I'm going to lose it! I turn on my heel and hurry to the refuge of the kitchen.

As I brown the ground turkey and carefully chop an onion my mom's words ring in my ears. I am sooo not a good girl. I am a selfish, self-centered coward! A good girl wouldn't stand by and let her best friends—past and present—be manipulated and deceived. A good girl would do the right thing and intervene, even if her best friends wouldn't thank her for it. Even if it meant they would hate her, cancel their New York plans, and sic all their nasty friends on her, a good girl would speak up!

Tears are now cascading down my face, but thankfully I can blame the onion. I chop the green pepper next, and then the mushrooms. Troy hates mushrooms, so I add lots. I'm just about to open the can of diced tomatoes when the doorbell rings.

"Troy!" my mom calls to my brother, who is playing computer games in the basement office.

"What!" he calls back.

"GET THE DOOR!" I yell down at him. God, anyone else would just automatically answer the door, but not my brother. I don't need to be within earshot to know he is calling me a fat bitch right now.

My head is buried in the narrow kitchen cupboard as I rummage for chili powder when Troy materializes behind me. "The door's for you," he says.

Extracting myself from the cupboard, I turn to face him. He's bouncing around like some sort of hyperactive puppy. "Who is it?"

My brother's face splits into an enormous smile. "Sienna Marshall."

Jeez, after everything that's happened he still has a crush on her? But this is just a fleeting thought. Obviously, the more pressing concern is, *What the hell is she doing here?*

With a deep, fortifying breath, I make my way to the door. "Hey," I say weakly.

"Hi," she says, smiling at me.

Her friendly manner takes me aback. "Uh...what are you doing here?"

"I was wondering if we could talk?"

Oh, here it comes. She knows about Daniel. And she knows I know. "Umm...sure. Do you want to come in?"

Sienna grimaces slightly, obviously remembering my dad's fortieth. "Not really."

Suddenly, my mom appears behind me. "Who's at the door, Lou—?" She stops when she sees the daughter of her nemesis. "Oh...hello, Sienna."

"Hi, Ms. Burroughs," she says, and I notice that she no longer feels comfortable calling her Denise.

"Sienna wants to talk to me," I say, turning to my mom with a desperate look.

"Okay, well, you're always welcome in our home, Sienna."

"Thanks, but..." She looks at me. "I thought maybe we could talk outside—or go for a walk or something?"

"Sure," I mumble, though my throat is closing with dread.

Outside, the September sky is still light. I'm thankful for this, as it makes it less likely that the evil triplets will be lurking in the shadows, waiting to jump me. I expect they'll prefer to torture me verbally, but I still can't rule out a physical attack. Silently, I follow Sienna down the front steps and to the end of our driveway. There, she stops and turns to face me. "This won't take long," she begins. "I just wanted to say that I know you heard me talking today."

"Uh...?" I decide it may be safest to play dumb.

"About the wedding and moving to New York with Daniel."

"Oh, right."

She pauses. "Well, I noticed that you looked like you were going to cry, and I realized that this must be really hard for you." My face must register my confusion as she elaborates. "I mean, you and I used to have big plans—Sienna Lou, design school and art school..."

I nod.

"I just hope that you'll still follow your dreams. Just because I'll be going to New York with Daniel instead of you, it doesn't mean that you can't still go. I think you should still apply to SVA. You're a really good artist. You'll totally get in."

"Thanks," I say, relief flooding over me. "I plan to. I'm moving there with my friend Russell."

"Good."

We stand silently for a moment, eyes on the ground in front of us. I'm just noticing that Sienna really does have fabulous taste in footwear when she says, "I know a lot of shit's gone down between us, but...I still think you deserve to be happy. You're a good person, Louise."

"Daniel's gay."

Sienna gapes at me and I swear the shock on her face is mirrored on my own. What the heck just happened? How could I just blurt something like that out? Have I got Tourette syndrome now? Wouldn't *that* just make my life even better!

Sienna gives an incredulous laugh. "What did you say?"

"Uh...nothing," I try.

"You did so," she snaps angrily. "What did you say?"

I know I'm defeated. I'll have to tell her everything, every sad, sordid detail about her boyfriend's betrayal. And I will do this with absolutely no regard for my own well-being. I guess Sienna and my mom are right: I am a good person...dammit!

"He's gay, Sienna," I say softly. "I saw him with Russell. They're seeing each other."

Her features turn hard. "I came here to try to be nice to you and this is how you thank me? You're sick, you know that?"

"I don't expect you to believe me. I know you'll go tell Daniel and he'll deny it. And I know you'll tell Audrey and everyone to be extra mean to me so that twelfth grade will be even worse than eleventh, but...you deserve to know. I hope..." I pause here, unsure what to say next. "I hope you'll at least look into it."

Sienna turns away from me and appears about to stalk off. But after a few seconds, she turns to face me again.

"Is Russell the guy who works at Orange Julius with you?"

"Yeah."

"And you're sure he's gay?"

"Trust me, I'm sure."

She bites her lip. "Daniel said they were friends from football camp."

I must not laugh. "Russell doesn't play football." As I watch Sienna process this information, I add, "I know you're not having sex with him."

She looks up. "Yeah, because *I* want to wait. Daniel's dying to do it with me."

"No, he's not," I say, feeling the sting of my words. "I'm sure the entire male population of Red Cedars is, but Daniel's not. He told me."

She snorts cruelly. "He told *you*? When have you even spoken to him?"

I tell her about our parking lot encounter, and how Daniel convinced me to keep his secret. "Look," I say gently, "you're not the first girl to fall for a gay guy." This was intended to be a sort of bonding moment, but Sienna shoots me a withering look. Obviously, my short crush on Russell does not compare to her much celebrated pre-engagement to Daniel.

Sienna is quiet for a moment, and I can see the wheels turning. So I decide to continue. "I found them at this look-out off of Highway 1A. I don't know where else they meet, but Daniel picks him up after work sometimes. You could always stake out the Willowbrook Mall parking lot... You know, if you want some proof."

"I don't need proof!" she snaps. "You're still bitter and angry because I dropped you as a friend, and now you're trying to ruin my happiness. You're pathetic, do you know that?"

"No, I'm not!" I reply, frustration overwhelming me. "I didn't want to get involved in this. Trust me, I didn't. But when I heard he gave you a promise ring, and that he's going to be in New York this summer..." I trail off. When I speak again, my voice is calmer, softer. "It was really nice of you to come here and see if I was okay, and when you said I was a good person...well, it was like I couldn't help but do the right thing. I just...had to tell you. I'm sorry."

Sienna's features are angry, but I notice a tear trickling slowly down the side of her nose. She looks about to say something, undoubtedly something like *Prepare to be destroyed.* Then she turns and walks away. I stand in the driveway and watch her get into her Toyota Rav 4 (another gift from her guilt-addled mother), which is parked at the curb. Without a backward glance, she speeds away.

When I walk back inside, my mom is hovering near the door. "What's going on? Is everything okay?"

"Yeah, it's fine," I say blandly. "I need to borrow your car."

"What for?" My mom asks, her voice filled with concern.

"I just need to talk to Russell." I look her directly in the eye. "I'll tell you everything later, but you don't need to worry."

To my surprise, this seems to work. Without another word, she moves to retrieve her keys from her purse.

When I arrive at Willowbrook Mall, I march directly to the Orange Julius stand. There's no point postponing the inevitable. I am about to lose my best friend and my job in one fell swoop. Obviously, once Jackie sees me in the mall when I'm supposedly sick, she'll have me fired. But what is unemployment compared to losing your best friend and being completely ostracized at school? At least I got my highlights done before the firing—not that they had the life-changing impact I had predicted.

But when I approach, Russell is alone, eating a hot dog. "Oh my god!" he says. "I thought you were sick!"

"I am...sort of. Where's Jackie?"

"I told her to take a break. It's still slow, and I couldn't stand listening to her moan about being called in on her night off. You might want to get out of here before she gets back."

"Right." Going to the side of the booth, I enter through the swinging doorway. "But I need to talk to you first."

Russell looks at me, his expression concerned. "Is everything okay?"

"No."

"Oh god!" he says, placing the hot dog on the counter and clasping his hands at his chest. Sure, *now* he seems effeminate.

"I told Sienna."

He hesitates. "About what?"

"About you and Daniel. He gave her a promise ring and they're moving to New York. I had to say something."

Slowly, Russell picks up his hot dog and tosses it in the trash. With his back to me, he looks out across the sparsely populated food court. I can't see the expression on his face, but I'm sure it is one of betrayal, anger, even rage. "I'm sorry," I manage to say.

Russell doesn't respond, but I see his shoulders rise and fall as he takes a deep breath. Finally, he turns to face me. "You said you'd stay out of it."

"I tried! But Sienna came to my house and she was being really nice to me and it just came out! It was like I couldn't control myself!"

"Yeah, that seems to be a problem with you."

Suddenly, I'm defensive. "It was the right thing to do," I say. "I couldn't stand by and watch him use her...and use you."

"I can take care of myself," Russell shoots back. "I don't need you taking care of me!"

I back down in the face of his anger. "I know. I screwed up. I totally understand if you hate me now."

Russell looks at me for a long moment. "I don't hate you. I could never hate you."

"Really?" I cry. "Never?"

"Well...don't test me."

"I won't," I assure him, reaching for his hand. "Are you okay?"

"Yeah, I knew it couldn't go on forever. I'm just really worried."

"About Daniel?"

"Yeah, about Daniel. He has so much pressure on him. I don't know how he's going to deal with this."

"What do you mean?" Worry brings a wobble to my voice. What will I do if Daniel goes berserk and ends up hurting himself? Or Sienna? Or his controlling parents? God, I hadn't even factored in that possibility. Like I'm not enough of a social leper without being the girl who outed

Daniel Noran and provoked his murderous rampage!

"I don't know what he'll do, but I don't think he's ready to be gay."

"Maybe he could just be bi?" I say hopefully.

Russell snorts. "Yeah, that would solve everything." Suddenly he gives me a shove toward the exit. "Here comes Jackie. You'd better get out of here."

As I scurry away, I call over my shoulder. "I'll call you later, okay?"

"Of course. Now go!" He shoos me away from the booth.

Neither Sienna nor Daniel is at school the next day. I try not to obsess about their absence over the weekend, but I can't help but worry. Thankfully, the evening news doesn't mention any murder-suicides. At school on Monday, I see Sienna in English Lit. She looks remarkably calm. Of course, she's not squealing and laughing her head off as usual, but she doesn't really look that upset. Despite the fact that she's not wearing her promise ring, my former BFF seems almost serene.

But Daniel Noran doesn't return to school all week. I'm dying to know what happened to him. Asking Sienna is out of the question. Despite our recent shows of affection, telling someone that their boyfriend is secretly gay does not bring you closer together. Finally, over after-work nachos with Russell, I learn the whole story.

"I saw Daniel last night," he says casually, focusing on the heaping plate of chips before us.

"You did? Is he okay?"

"He's fine. He said it went okay with Sienna. She was upset, but really nice about it, actually."

"That's good. What about his parents?"

"They still don't know. Sienna's not going to tell anyone. It's not exactly flattering for either of them."

"I guess not. But if everything's okay, why hasn't he been at school?"

"His dad had been pressuring him to go to this fancy, all-boys boarding school in Montreal. He's decided to spend twelfth grade there."

"Really?"

Russell laughs. "Daniel seems to think if he's away from me, he'll miraculously become straight again."

"At an all-boys boarding school?"

"I know! If anything, it's going to make him *gayer*!"

I place my hand on top of his. "Are you going to miss him?"

"Yeah," he says sadly, "it was fun while it lasted, but I knew it would end at some point."

I hate to make this all about me, but I have to ask. "And you don't blame me?"

Russell gives me an exasperated look. "No, I don't blame you. Besides, we've got to focus on our plans. I've got to get a demo CD together and contact some clubs, and you've got to get your applications in."

"I know," I say thankfully. "We've got to look forward, not back!"

Russell holds up his glass of Diet Coke. "To looking forward!" he says jubilantly. "To the future!"

"To the future!" I say, clinking my glass to his.

👀👀

And that is how I'll get through my last year of school: by looking to the future. Not that twelfth grade could possibly be as painful and humiliating as eleventh. I feel fairly confident that my parents have caused me enough embarrassment for one lifetime. I mean, what are the odds that my dad and, say, Leah Montgomery's mom are going to get it on in front of my brother? Slim to none, I'd say—especially given that Leah's mom appears to be in her mid-fifties and has a rather thick moustache. And I doubt my mom will leave Dave to get knocked up by any of my other teachers. So, if I focus on our move to New York, I just might survive senior year.

Since Sienna and I have reached a sort of silent truce and the evil triplets are no longer torturing me, there's even a chance I might enjoy my final months at Red Cedars. Mr. Sumner is going to announce this year's theater production soon, and I'm very excited about it. I'm becoming increasingly interested in a career in the theater—or maybe even film. Now that I'm no longer on the periphery of the popular crowd, I don't have to pretend to be cool and blasé about my interests. I'm free from the constraints that once bound me! Free to have passions outside of boys, belts, and earrings. Of course, I would really like to get my hair highlighted again.

As I enter the lobby on Monday, I notice Sienna and her crowd occupying their usual spot near the stairs. Daniel is absent, of course, but there are a number of interchangeable, good-looking guys milling about. Out of habit, I turn my face away and quicken my pace before remembering that I no longer have anything to fear from them. Consciously, I relax my gait.

"Louise!" I hear my name and turn toward the source. Sienna stands up and comes toward me. For the briefest moment, I'm filled with dread, but the small smile on her face assures me everything is okay.

"Hey," I say as she approaches.

"Hey." With a small movement of her head, she indicates that we should continue walking to my locker. "So..." she says as we move through the foyer, "Daniel's going to Selwyn House in Montreal."

"I heard." I look at her. "Russell saw him before he left."

Sienna bites her lip and nods her head. "I know." She stops walking. "I didn't want to believe you, but I know you don't lie. And when I thought about it, it did explain a lot of things."

Of course I'm dying to know what things, but she is not forthcoming. As we begin to walk again, Sienna says, "So...I've been watching *Project Runway*, and it seems you have to be able to draw to go to fashion design school. I was wondering if you could give me some tips one day after school." She gives me a hopeful smile.

"Sure." I smile back. "But we'll meet on neutral territory, right?"

Sienna laughs. "Definitely! I was thinking Starbucks."

"Sounds good."

Sienna stops walking and faces me. She almost looks like she wants to hug me or something. That would be really corny, I guess, but I actually wouldn't mind. But popular girls don't make such cheesy gestures. Instead, Sienna says, "Thanks...I'll catch up with you later." Then she heads back to the in-crowd.

I continue on to my locker with a sense of contentment. Sienna and I will never have the friendship we once had, but I'm okay with that. In fact, I wouldn't want to go back to the way things were. It's a relief not to be a part of her clique, pretending to have common interests with her other friends. But maybe Sienna and I can have a different kind of friendship.

When I reach my locker, I open my combination lock and stuff my backpack inside. I'm hanging up my jacket when I become aware of someone beside me. Turning, I feel my breath catch in my throat. Aaron Hansen is back, and like some kind of miraculous gift from the heavens, he has grown at least four inches over the summer! God, he's really filled out too. He must have gained about twenty pounds!

"Hi, Louise," he says with that same lazy smile that, now that he's about five-eleven, could probably qualify as sexy!

"A—Aaron," I stammer, "you're back."

"Yeah," he closes his locker. "How was your summer?"

"Uh, it was fine...good." I close my locker too. "How was Chicago?"

"It was fantastic!" he says, his eyes lighting up. "I learned so much, and it was great working with a professional theater troupe. I think I can bring a lot to this year's production. You're going to be our set designer again, aren't you?"

"Yeah," I reply brightly, marveling at how broad his shoulders have become.

Aaron continues as we wander down the hall toward homeroom. "That's great. Have you heard when Mr. Sumner's going to announce what play we're doing?"

Yes...I just might enjoy this year after all.

Acknowledgments

Thank you to my editor, Pam Robertson, for her wisdom, support and guidance. Thank you to everyone at Annick Press for bringing this book into being. And thank you to John, Ethan and Tegan—for always being in my corner, and always making me laugh.

About the Author

Robyn Harding grew up in Quesnel, a logging town in northern British Columbia. She published her first adult novel, *The Journal of Mortifying Moments*, in 2004. Since then, she's published three more novels: *The Secret Desires of a Soccer Mom*, *Unravelled*, and *Chronicles of a Midlife Crisis*.

Robyn lives in Vancouver, B.C. with her husband, kids, and a very small, completely frivolous dog named Ozzie.